D1412710

67

RT

CUT ONE, THEY ALL BLEED

Marshal Collier yelled, and lunged away from the buxom blonde at his side.

From the corner of his eye as he began the movement, Collier saw Madam Bulldog was stepping in the opposite direction and reaching for her Webley. Hoping the teller was showing an equal grasp of the situation, he did not dare spare so much as a glance to make sure. Nor could he waste time considering the possible repercussions should he kill the dandily-dressed relation of Frank Cousins.

Brock Cousins saw Collier's movement, and realised that he had brought danger on himself by looking away. Alarmed, he quickly raised the barrel of his Colt and fired . . .

CUT ONE,
THEY ALL BLEED

J. T. EDSON

This first edition published in Great Britain 1987 by
SEVERN HOUSE PUBLISHERS LTD of
40–42 William IV Street, London WC2N 4DF
by arrangement with Transworld Publishers Ltd

British Library Cataloguing in Publication Data
Edson, J. T.
Cut one, they all bleed.
I. Title
823′.914 [F]   PR6055.D8
ISBN 0–7278–1411–7

Printed and bound in Great Britain

*For Joe Chapler, who speaks
Hungarian better than any
other Englishman I know.*

AUTHOR'S NOTE

While complete in itself, this title follows the events recorded in: THE HIDE AND HORN SALOON. Some of the incidents recorded in both volumes previously appeared under the title, Part One, 'Better Than Calamity', THE WILD-CATS. However, the Counter family have agreed that the full story can at last be put into print. They made the stipulation that the two books must be included in the Calamity Jane and not the Floating Outfit series, as was formerly the case, which we have done.

To save our 'old hands' from repetition, but for the benefit of new readers, we have recorded details of the careers of Miss Martha 'Calamity Jane' Canary and Mark Counter, along with those references to Old West terms and events about which we are most regularly requested for information in the form of Appendices.

While we realize that in our present 'permissive' society, we would include the actual profanities used by various people in the narrative, we do not concede that a spurious desire for 'realism' is any excuse to do so.

Lastly, as we do not pander to the current 'trendy' usage of the metric system, except where the calibres of certain firearms—i.e. Walther P-38, 9mm—are concerned, we will continue to employ miles, yards, feet, inches, pounds and ounces when referring to distances and weights.

J.T. Edson

Active member, Western Writers of America,
Melton Mowbray, Leics., England.

CHAPTER ONE

I Don't Approve Of Bribery

'Hey now, god-damn it!' growled the elderly deputy town marshal, coming from the office in the front section of the Benson City jailhouse which he had just entered and glaring truculently at the only occupant of the four cells at the rear of the building. 'What the hell's all that hootin' 'n' hollerin' about?'

Even seated upon the hard and uncomfortable narrow wooden bunk, which was practically the sole furnishing for his place of incarceration, the prisoner conveyed the impression of being massive in proportions. On rising in an apparently languid fashion, he confirmed that the suggestion of bulk was not merely an illusion.

Two inches over six foot, in his early twenties, Trudeau Front de Boeuf—although that was not the name by which he was known in the small Texas range town—was built on lines of vastly greater than average size. He had soft and wavy brown hair which was allowed to grow somewhat longer than was considered acceptable among cowhands.[1] Not that anything in his appearance or attire suggested he might belong to such a hard riding, hard working and harder playing fraternity. Rather the garments he had on implied he was a successful professional gambler, or wished to give the impression of being one. There was a pallor to his handsome, if somewhat petulant features which would have been re-

1. *See* Footnote 4, APPENDIX THREE. *J.T.E.*

11

placed by a tan had he spent any length of time working cattle in the open air and his large, well kept hands would have become rougher if such was his vocation. However, while he filled his frilly bosomed mauve silk shirt, glossy floral patterned black vest and tight legged off-white trousers tightly, his bulk was formed of hard and firm flesh rather than soft and flabby tissue.

'I was just about to ask you that very same thing,' the prisoner claimed, standing upon spread apart feet encased in Hersome gaiter boots and fingering a neatly tied black silk cravat. His tone was quiet and seemingly meek, with the accent of a well educated Southron born somewhere other than Texas in what had formerly been the Confederate States of America. 'But it's no use you shouting for the marshal. He hasn't been in all evening, not even to bring me my supper.'

'To hell with you and your son-of-a-bitching supper!' the peace officer barked malevolently, although aware that the prisoner's mother had paid for him to receive better food than was supplied to others held in the jail. 'I've just got word Frank Cousins's fixing to bring his gang in tonight, looking for evens 'cause that god-damned brother-in-law of his'n got made wolf bait down to the Drover's Saloon a couple of weeks back!'

'Who killed him?' Front de Boeuf inquired, judging from the various sounds coming in through the barred window of his cell that "word" of the impending visit had not been restricted to the deputy.

'Me 'n' the marshal,' the peace officer replied.

'Lordy lord, that was somewhat *tactless* of you and the marshal, now wasn't it?' the bulky young man suggested, his manner mildly sardonic. He knew that the two members of the local law enforcement agency were far from diligent in the performance of their duties, even though they had taken him into custody. 'What is it they say about Frank Cousins and his clan?'

'Huh?' grunted the deputy, looking puzzled.

'Isn't it something like, if you cut one, they all bleed?' Front de Boeuf elaborated, still fingering the cravat.

12

'Yeah, that's what they say,' the elderly peace officer admitted and made a wry face. Such was his perturbation that he was more loquacious than usual and he went on, 'Trouble being, nobody'd gotten 'round to letting us know who the son-of-a-bitch was. So, reckoning he wasn't nothing more'n just another no-account cow-nurse, me 'n' the marshal just natural' cut him down.'

'*Naturally*,' the prisoner said drily. 'Only, as you would put it, "trouble being", now his uncle and all their gang are coming with the intention of wreaking vengeance upon you, the marshal and the town.'

'That's the word I've been give'!'

'I've heard it said they're most *thorough* on such occasions.'

'And me!' the peace officer confirmed, losing the derisive attitude that he generally adopted when addressing the prisoner.

'So what are *you* going to do about it?' Front de Boeuf queried, the change in the deputy's demeanour not having escaped his notice.

'Tell the marshal what's doing, happen I can find out where he's at. I was just headed out to look for him when you started yelling.'

'And, after you've told him, or without telling him if he isn't *very* easy to find, you're going to collect your horse and put as many miles as possible between you and the Cousins' gang?'

'I sure's hell's for sinners am!' the peace officer stated, his manner defiant. 'God damn it, I'm way too old to start trading lead with a bunch of gun-handy owlhoots like he'll have with him.'

'There are some who might say it's your duty and what you are paid to do,' Front de Boeuf pointed out.

'Duty my ass!' the deputy spat back. ' 'Specially when every other son-of-a-bitch in this stinking one-hoss town's already running scared 'n' wouldn't back the marshal even *should* he conclude to stick around and make a fight of it.

Which, knowing him like I do, there's more chance a snowball'd stay frozed up in hell than he'll do *that*.'

'And where does that leave me?'

'How do you mean?'

'From what I've heard, Cousins had the jail burned to the ground when he and his men raided Narrow Forks last year to avenge a cousin who had been hanged there,' Front de Boeuf explained. 'And, as I'm being held prisoner in this one, I can't say the prospect fills me with wild enthusiasm.'

'That's all your misfortune and none of my own, Mr. Cholmundersley, or whichever god-damned way you say it,' the deputy declared.

'It's pronounced, "Chumley",' the young man explained, having adopted the alias, "Barrington Cholmondeley" for the visit to Benson City.

'I don't give shit how you say it!' the peace officer growled. 'Happen you hadn't got caught out as a god-damned cheating tinhorn, you wouldn't've got put here in the first place!'

'There's *some* truth in that,' Front de Boeuf conceded, without bothering to deny the reason given for his incarceration or to point out he was held because his mother had declined to pay a bribe which would have had the charges against him dropped. 'Of course, breaking the jaw of the mayor's favourite son could have had something to do with it too.'

'That, 'long of you busting up them other three rich young fellers when they didn't take kind' to you fleecing 'em,' supplemented the elderly deputy. 'Then damned near wrecking the Drovers afore me 'n' the marshal could get there to bring you in for disturbing the peace.'

'I can't gainsay that's what I was doing when you arrived,' Front de Boeuf admitted, as if conferring a favour. 'The trouble is, as I tried to explain to the judge, I'm inclined to be somewhat highly strung when I'm excited and I have this tendency to get excited when I'm accused of cheating at cards.' ·

14

'I'd say you was more'n just *accused*!' the peace officer objected. 'That deck's you'd used to clean 'em out was thumb-nailed so good we couldn't barely see the marks. Which none of them college-taught, fancy-pants young yahoos playing 'gain' you was close to smart enough to've knowed how to do it and that only left *you*.'

'A most reasonable assumption, put that way,' the massive young man drawled and, as he had already done so, he made no further attempt to disclaim responsibility for the deck of cards having been marked by being scratched with a thumb nail during play. Instead, seeing the peace officer was turning away, he picked up the wide brimmed, low crowned, white "planter's" hat from where it lay with his expensive black broadcloth tail coat on the bunk and continued, 'I don't suppose you would consider letting me out of here?'

'You don't *consider* son-of-a-bitching right,' the deputy confirmed, but halted his turn and looked over his shoulder.

'Not even if I was to offer to pay *you* my fine?' Front de Boeuf hinted.

'The judge didn't fast fix no fine with his favourite son having got took home with a bust jaw and three stove-in ribs,' the peace officer answered. 'He said thirty days in the hoosegow and'd've likely made it more happen that fancy and high-toned momma of your'n hadn't been looking pretty at him in the courthouse—Or, which being, maybe even less, 'cepting his missus was in town and it was *her* favourite son's well's you'd tromped, whomped 'n' stom—!' The mocking words trailed away as he saw what was happening in the cell and he swung around swiftly, saying, 'Where the hell did you get *that* from?'

'In here,' Front de Boeuf answered, gesturing with a one hundred dollar bill towards the sweat band inside the crown of the hat.

'God damn it!' the deputy ejaculated, eyeing the money avariciously. 'We searched you when we brought you in!'

'But not well enough, obviously,' the young man asserted, tossing the hat on to the bunk and holding the bill in plain

15

view between the tips of his left thumb and forefinger. 'Anyway, that is hardly the point right now. I don't suppose they pay you over-generously and you could probably use some extra money to keep you going until you find another town that needs a deputy.'

'Yeah!' the peace officer grunted pensively.

'The—*fine*, shall we call it?—would help,' Front de Boeuf went on, watching and listening with considerable interest to the way in which the other was reacting. 'Don't you think so too?'

'*Yeah*!' the peace office repeated vehemently, the sum being more than double the pay he received from the town each month. 'Hand it over!'

'*After* I'm outside the cell,' the young man answered.

'Hand the son-of-a-bitch over!' the deputy snarled, pulling his Colt 1860 Army Model revolver from its holster.

'*After* you've let me out of the cell, as I said,' the prisoner replied, showing not the slightest concern as the weapon was cocked and pointed at him through the bars of the door. 'And, *please*, don't waste both our time threatening me with that.'

'I ain't just *threatening*, god-damn it!' the elderly deputy warned. 'I'll *use* the son-of-a-bitch!'

'Go ahead, if you're that *stupid*,' Front de Boeuf offered, his manner calm and completely lacking in fear. 'You've no idea where the marshal might be, or how soon he could be coming back. If he hears a shot, it will fetch him in here *muy pronto*. Then you'll have to at least *share* the money with him. Or, even more likely, going by what I've seen of him, he could decide to take it *all* as you won't be the only one needing travelling money.'

'Could be he ain't nowheres near close enough to hear the shot,' the deputy countered, although he was in agreement over the way in which his superior would regard the bill being exhibited to him.

'There is that possibility,' Front de Boeuf drawled, but with no indication of being disturbed or alarmed by the

16

thought of this proving to be the case. 'It all depends upon whether *you* want to take the chance he isn't near by. However, on the other hand—!'

'On the other hand, *what*?' the peace officer was unable to prevent himself from inquiring when the comment was not completed.

'You don't need to share with him at all and there is more money for the—*fine*—if need be.'

'Where?'

'Hidden where you would have to spend much more time than you dare gamble on having if you try to find it,' Front de Boeuf claimed, exuding complete confidence. 'You missed this bill, don't forget.'

'How much more of a *fine* is it to be?' the deputy asked.

'I can go another hundred,' the young man offered.

'Let me see the son-of-a-bitch!' the peace officer demanded, gesturing with the revolver in what he hoped would be the commanding fashion of one still in full control of the situation.

'Not until I see you holding the key for the cell,' Front de Boeuf asserted, his manner indicating there would be no compromise on the subject as far as he was concerned. 'And I would like to point out that time is passing while you are standing there trying, without the *slightest* chance of success I can assure you, to force me to change my mind.'

'All right, you god-damned, smart-assed son-of-a-bitch!' the deputy snarled, conceding defeat with bad grace. 'You get it out and have it ready to show me when I come back with the keys and god help you happen you can't.'

Watching the elderly peace officer slouching into the office, a smile came which changed the face of the young prisoner. It caused him to lose the impression of something close to petulant innocence which had frequently led people to form misconceptions and discount him as a 'momma's boy', under the thumb of a domineering mother. At that moment, looking after the deputy, his expression was such it gave a hint of the Norman stock from which the paternal side

17

of his family had sprung.[2] Once more reaching into the sweat band of the hat, he removed another of the five one hundred dollar bills transferred there from the hollow heel of his right boot after he had been searched by the marshal and deputy prior to being put into the cell. Putting on the hat and resuming the innocuous expression, he was displaying the two banknotes when the elderly peace officer returned.

'Here they are,' Front de Boeuf announced, stepping to the window and raising the hand holding the money so it was between the bars.

'So I can see,' the deputy answered, his tone sour as he realized the implications of the action. Gesturing with the bunch of keys in his left hand and still holding the Colt in the right, he went on, 'All right, I'll open up.'

'And I'll give you the money as soon as I'm outside,' the young man promised, going to pick up the broadcloth coat. However, although he shook it fastidiously, he did not don it. Instead, carrying it over his arm, he walked forward after the door was unlocked and opened, continuing in the same mildly even tone, 'Thank you for your *kindness*, sir. You won't be the loser by it.'

'I don't aim to be,' the peace officer claimed, his voice menacing, having withdrawn a few steps and keeping the revolver in alignment. 'Hand 'em over!'

'Certainly,' Front de Boeuf assented, in what appeared to be an amiably submissive voice, extending his left hand.

. Releasing his hold as the deputy was reaching greedily for the bills, the massive young man set them at liberty before they could be taken from him. As they were fluttering downwards, the peace officer followed their movements with his gaze. In doing so, he allowed the barrel of the revolver to

2. *The researches of fictionist-genealogist Philip José Farmer—author of, among numerous other titles,* TARZAN ALIVE, A Definitive Biography Of Lord Greystoke *and* DOC SAVAGE, His Apocalyptic Life—*have established that Trudeau Front de Boeuf was descended from Reginald of that name, lord of Torquilstone Castle during the reign of Richard the 1st of England. See:* IVANHOE, *by Sir Walter Scott. J.T.E.*

waver until it was no longer pointing at the broad chest of the prisoner.

Instantly, displaying a speed far different from his close to somnolent movements until that moment, Front de Boeuf swung his right arm around and up. Caught at the side of the head with a backhand slap, such was its force that the elderly deputy was flung across the cell block. Falling from his grasp, the cocked Colt landed without discharging. The deputy, rebounding from the wall, joined the weapon on the floor and lay motionless.

'I've been waiting to do that ever since I was put in here,' the young man remarked casually, although his victim could not hear what he was saying. 'And, while I said you wouldn't be the loser by setting me free, as I don't approve of bribery when I'm the one who is being made to pay it, the *gain* will be all you deserve, you miserable, unpleasant and dishonest old bastard.'

Having retrieved the money while delivering the sentiment, Front de Boeuf strolled without so much as a second glance at the man he had struck down into the office. Nor, being the kind of person he was, would he have shown any greater concern if his elderly victim had behaved in a less obnoxious fashion than had proved to be the case during the period of their acquaintance. Nevertheless, he did derive a certain amount of satisfaction from the thought that he had repaid the numerous insults and indignities he had suffered at the hands of the malevolent old peace officer since his arrest and the refusal of his mother to purchase his freedom.

Looking cautiously around as he was emerging from the rear section of the jailhouse, the bulky young man went to the desk in the centre, which was almost invariably an item of furniture in the office of every type of law enforcement agency west of the Mississippi River. Aware that only the marshal and the deputy were employed to keep the peace in Benson City, he was not surprised to find he had the room to himself. Nor was he challenged by anybody as he tossed his coat on to the desk and, trying the deep drawer on the left into which his property had been placed when he was arrested, he found it was locked.

Instead of taking the time to collect the bundle of keys which were still dangling from the door of the cell, Front de Boeuf grasped the handle of the drawer. Bracing his right knee against the side, he gave a sudden and powerful wrench. As further evidence of the power his massive yet lethargic-seeming body could exert, to the accompaniment of the sharp click of snapping metal as the lock was broken, it opened. Removing the pocketbook bound in expensive 'morocco' leather, he checked its few contents were intact. Replacing the money from his hat, he turned his attention to retrieving the rest of his belongings. Even if he hadn't known he might soon be needing some of the items, having paid a high price for having them prepared as aids for the protection of himself and his mother in their nefarious and far from innocent way of life, he would have refused to leave them behind.

Picking up the ivory handled, fancily etched Colt Pocket Pistol of Navy Calibre—sometimes erroneously called the 'Model of 1853' and a revolver despite its name—with a four inch barrel, the young man checked that the five chambers of its cylinder were still capped and loaded. Satisfied it was ready to be fired if the need should arise, he slipped it into the leather-lined slot at the left side of his fancy vest so the butt pointed forward. With that done, he set about reclaiming the rest of his armament.

First, Front de Boeuf lifted from the drawer a harness comprised of a broad leather strap to which a longer and more slender webbing loop was attached. Hooking his left arm through the latter, so it passed across his wide back, he eased the former over his right shoulder and settled it comfortably. Then he put on the long coat and concealed it from view.

Having completed the preparations for carrying it, the young man collected his Greener ten gauge shotgun from the drawer. It was, however, far different from when it had left the well known manufacturer in England. The twin Damascus twist barrels had been cut down to approximately ten inches in length and the stock was removed behind the wrist of the butt. This was rounded and smoothed into a configuration resembling the grip of a flintlock pistol from the Eighteenth Century. Offering a more secure hold to fight the recoil when being fired, although retaining something of its original shape, the wooden foregrip had been shortened slightly. Reduced to about eighteen inches overall, with the weight lowered to around seven pounds, it was further modified to perform the specialized functions of what was known as a 'whipit' gun. Threaded into the barrel rib, exactly at the point of balance, was a brass eyebolt.

Breaking open the whipit gun and finding it was unloaded, Front de Boeuf inserted two of the half a dozen brass shells from the drawer and pocketed the remainder. Closing the breech and drawing aside the long right flap of the broadcloth coat, he slid the head of the eyebolt into the metal slot on the bottom of the leather shoulder strap. Turning the shortened barrels downwards, he retained the deadly weapon in a horizontal position and, releasing the garment, caused it to be held there. When it was needed, opening the coat would allow it to tilt until vertical and ready to be brought out and fired.

Having regained possession of everything taken from him, the young man glanced at the entrance to the cell area. No sound came from inside it. Concluding the elderly peace officer was still unconscious, he did not offer to ascertain whether his supposition was correct or if his blow might have produced an even more serious effect. Satisfied the marshal would have other things than his escape to worry about shortly, even if his blow had killed the deputy, he went to the front door and opened it. Checking in each direction, he stepped outside when sure he would not be seen by anybody who might challenge his right to leave.

CHAPTER TWO

As Usual, It Is Left To Me

Moving with a leisurely-seeming gait, which nevertheless carried him swiftly along the rough planks of the sidewalk, Trudeau Front de Boeuf continuously glanced about him. He decided the entire population of Benson City was taking seriously the 'word' received by the deputy town marshal. None of the business premises on the short main street were open. Even the Drovers Saloon, which would normally at least be lit up at eight o'clock in the evening, was silent and in darkness. Nor was anybody to be seen. Although there were sounds of activity elsewhere, these sounds were more suggestive of alarm than normal behaviour.

All of which, the massive young man told himself, was testimony of the fear inspired even by the name of the man said to be coming to avenge the killing of his brother-in-law by the marshal and deputy.

Ostensibly a honest and prosperous rancher, Frank Cousins had a much more sinister and well deserved reputation. Although it was rumoured that the large crew he hired were cold blooded outlaws rather than cowhands and earned their pay from various illicit enterprises, nothing had ever been proven. What few attempts had been made to do so had failed due to the lack of positive evidence. The refusal of witnesses to testify had been created by the fear Cousins had taken care to ensure his name inspired. This had arisen out of the way he reacted, no matter what the circumstances, should any member of his numerous clan be harmed. Nor did he

22

restrict his reprisals to those directly responsible, but struck hard and ruthlessly at the town or ranch where the incident had taken place. Having done so, he would have his attorney proclaim his innocence and declare enemies were seeking to discredit him. If brought before a Grand Jury, as had happened occasionally when protests reached such a pitch that the soon to be replaced Reconstruction Administration were compelled to take action, the realization that reprisals would follow prevented sufficient people entering the witness box and no indictment could be obtained.[1]

On arriving at the Central Hotel, a grandiloquent and misleading title as it was the only establishment of its kind in Benson City, Front de Boeuf found the lobby to be empty although illuminated by hanging lamps. Passing the reception desk, without the clerk putting in an appearance, he went upstairs to the second floor. This too was lit and he strode rapidly along the passage towards the adjoining rooms occupied by his mother and himself. As he was approaching her quarters, the door opened and a masculine figure emerged.

Tall, burly, surly featured and middle-aged, the man leaving the room gave indications that his business had been somewhat more intimate than merely social or business. There was a smudge of something red on the collar of his grubby white shirt which was unlikely to have been present on his arrival, nor produced by anything in his possession. While the vest of his cheap brown three-piece suit was fastened, two buttons on the fly of his trousers had been missed when it was last closed. He was carrying a none too clean derby hat and had on a gunbelt with a Colt 1860 Army revolver in the holster tied to his right thigh by a pigging thong.

Even without needing to see the tarnished silver badge of

1. 'Grand Jury': under the legal system of the United States of America, a special jury formed of a statutory number of citizens—usually more than twelve—to investigate accusations against persons charged with crime and indict them for trial before a 'petit' jury if there is sufficient evidence. J.T.E.

office pinned to the vest, Front de Boeuf recognized his mother's departing guest!

What was more, if the marshal's response to the sight of the former prisoner was any guide, the recognition was mutual!

Letting out a profanely startled exclamation, regardless of what he had been doing in the room, the town marshal dropped his hat and grabbed for the Colt!

Knowing his mother was far from averse to masculine company and did not restrict it to a mere platonic relationship, even at short acquaintance, Front de Boeuf was neither shocked nor annoyed by the implications that she had been indulging in an intimate association with a man. Furthermore, having no doubt she had had a perfectly sound reason for selecting such an uncouth person as the departing guest, he would not have raised any objections over her latest companion being the peace officer responsible for his arrest and incarceration. However, the way in which the marshal was behaving warned that he could not dismiss the visit as casually as would otherwise have been the case. Nor, he suspected, would he be allowed to offer an explanation for his presence even if he could think up anything satisfactory.

Despite having considerable proficiency in their respective use, the bulky young man did not attempt to reach for either of the weapons he had retrieved from the desk at the jailhouse. Instead, he bunched and drove forward his left fist with a precision many a professional pugilist would have envied. It struck the marshal just below the *solar plexus*, doubling him at the waist before he could do anything more than grasp the butt of his Colt.

Flung into the room by the far from gentle impact, the peace officer was allowed no chance to recover and complete his draw. Striding swiftly across the threshold, Front de Boeuf swung up his right leg with an alacrity equal to that with which the punch had been delivered. Caught under the jaw by the toe of the Hersome gaiter boot, the marshal was lifted erect and precipitated to crash on his back alongside the bed he had recently been occupying most enjoyably with the

24

mother of his assailant. Returning to the passage, Front de Boeuf listened for a moment. Then, giving a nod of satisfaction, he closed the door. At any other time, the commotion caused by his victim landing on the floor might have been heard downstairs and investigated. There was no indication of this happening, probably because all the staff of the hotel had fled to their homes.

'Great heavens to Betsy!' Jessica Front de Boeuf ejaculated, rising from the chair at the dressing-table where she had been carrying out repairs to the damage her make-up had suffered during the session of passionate love-play she had not long brought to an end. Her voice, a rich contralto with a pronounced and cultured Southron accent, took on the note of asperity which frequently came when she addressed her only offspring. 'And just what in the name of the Good Lord do you think you're doing?' she demanded.

'I got out of jail—!' the young man began.

'I can see that for myself!' the woman interrupted imperiously. Turning, she indicated the sprawled-out, motionless marshal with a wave of her heavily jewelled right hand, and continued just as heatedly, 'And, as I had just learned all we need from *that* and persuaded him to set you free in the morning, I hope you haven't *escaped*!'

Looking at the speaker, even a stranger would have guessed from where the young man had come by his size and bulk!

Having married at seventeen—although, to annoy and embarrass her family for having disowned her, she now, when not using an alias, employed her maiden name instead of that of her long abandoned husband—with the urgent need of being six months into pregnancy, Jessica Front de Boeuf was still an imposing figure of a woman. Five foot nine in height, she had a richly Junoesque body which a life of little restraint had not yet contrived to destroy the curvaceous fullness of her 'hourglass' figure. The texture of the skin was beginning to coarsen a trifle, but her olive skinned face was beautiful if marred by lines which indicated an arrogant and domineering nature. Due to having been deserted by the

25

latest of a sequence of maids who had found her temper and infrequency of payment intolerable, her black hair was not quite so elegantly coiffured as usual. Still unfastened at the back, the dress she wore was stylish and revealing to the point of being risqué. As far as could be seen, which was to just below waist level, she wore no undergarments beneath it. While her feet were also bare, she had either just donned or kept on the jewellery which glistened about her neck, in the lobes of her ears, and on her wrists and hands.

'Well?' the woman snapped, as her son crossed to look out of the window instead of responding to her comment.

'I have escaped, momma,' Front de Boeuf admitted, turning around.

'Whatever for, damn it?' Jessica challenged, placing hands on her hips and thrusting forward a plentifully endowed bosom. 'I had *that* eating out of my hand—!'

'So you've found out what we needed to know?'

'Of course and, as I said, he'd agreed to let you go in the morning.'

'I'm afraid we can't wait until then before leaving,' the young man asserted, stepping over the unconscious peace officer as he strode towards the wardrobe. 'But not because of him, or that old deputy I left at the jailhouse—!'

'Then why, in heavens name, did you decide you had to escape?' Jessica interrupted, patience never having been her strong point.

'I know you're friendly with Frank Cousins, momma,' Front de Boeuf replied. 'But he might not be around when some of the scum he has riding for him see your jewellery.'

'What do you mean?'

'It seems your friend, the marshal, and his deputy, were sufficiently ill-advised as to kill a brother-in-law of Cousins in the belief he was merely a cowhand. And you know what they say ab—!'

'*That* didn't say anything about it!' Jessica protested, once again indicating the recumbent peace officer. 'And excellent *company* as I know I am, it isn't likely he would have overlooked anything of such importance.'

26

'He didn't know what was coming, or at least when,' Front de Boeuf explained, opening the door of the wardrobe. 'The deputy had only just heard the news and was looking for him to pass it on.'

'He did say it sounded as if something might be wrong,' the woman claimed pensively. 'That was how I was able to get rid of him. I suggested he should go and see what was happening, then come back if it was nothing important.'

'It's far from being "nothing important", momma,' the massive young man assessed, lifting a portmanteau from the wardrobe.

'You're right,' Jessica agreed. 'As you say, Frank and I are on good terms, but it might be some of his men who don't know that who come upon us. I know he would punish whoever molested me, but that wouldn't make me feel much better over it having happened.' She gave an indignant sniff as another thought struck her and went on, 'Mr. Thompson won't be best pleased with the Cousins' crowd, though.'

'I suppose he won't momma,' Front de Boeuf said. 'Particularly as you have all he wanted to know.'

One of the ways through which the unscrupulous pair augmented their income was by acquiring information for robberies otherwise unobtainable by known outlaws. They had been commissioned by 'Smokey' Hill Thompson to scout the bank in Benson City so he and his gang could hold it up.[2] Although the trouble at the Drovers Saloon had not been envisaged, Jessica had seen how her son's fight would offer her a reason for remaining in the small town. That was why she had not done anything earlier to obtain the release of her son from the jailhouse.

'Oh well, we've done *our* part and Thompson can't blame us for what Cousins does,' the woman remarked philosophically, starting to remove instead of fastening the dress. 'Go and collect your things, then you can pack for me while I'm changing.'

2. *Some information about 'Smokey' Hill Thompson is given in:* THE MAKING OF A LAWMAN. *J.T.E.*

Returning to the passage, Front de Boeuf could not hear any activity elsewhere in the hotel. Knowing he and his mother were the only guests, unless others had arrived while he was in jail, he concluded they had the place to themselves. Unlocking the door, with the key which had been left in his coat pocket, he entered his room. In accordance with their usual precautions against the need for making a hurried departure, which were necessitated by their way of life, he had unpacked only the bare essentials on arrival. Replacing these in the bulky portmanteau which held such of his possessions as were not on his person, he picked it up and left.

As he expected, on reaching his mother's quarters, the young man found she had wasted no time. Already the dress lay on the bed and she was tucking an unfastened white silk blouse into the waist of the skirt of an elegant black two-piece travelling costume. Making no attempt to cover her otherwise exposed naked torso, she told him to put away the discarded garment.

Being equally aware that a hurried departure might be called for as a result of some indiscretion on the part of one or the other of them, Jessica had kept out only what was needed from her portmanteau and steamer trunk. Having been required to perform such a task on numerous occasions when no maid or other help was available, the young man folded and packed away the dress in a competent fashion. While his mother was fastening the blouse and donning the jacket, he collected the box in which she had placed the majority of her jewellery and concealed it amongst the garments in the portmanteau.

'Thank heavens we have our own transport,' Jessica remarked, on completion of her dressing. 'But I don't suppose there will be a bell boy to carry our baggage to the livery barn?'

'No, momma,' Front de Boeuf replied. 'The lobby and everywhere else downstairs was deserted when I came through and it still doesn't sound any different.'

'Then at least we won't have to pay for our rooms,' the

28

woman commented and nodded to where the peace officer was groaning and stirring slightly. 'Let's leave before he recovers his senses, not that they are *much* when he has them.'

'They weren't, momma,' Front de Boeuf answered, swinging the big trunk on to his left shoulder with an ease indicative of his considerable strength. Taking his portmanteau in his right hand, he continued, 'Even without the Cousins' gang being on its way, he won't be in any condition to come after us before we leave town and neither will his deputy.'

'Blast it!' the woman snorted, never caring to carry out anything she regarded as a menial task. 'If only Edward was here, I wouldn't have to do this!'

In the absence of Edward Kinsella—who was obsessively devoted to her but who had been sent to scout the bank in another town for Thompson—or any other assistance, Jessica picked up her own portmanteau and a reticule. Proving she was far from a weakling, her elegant demeanour notwithstanding, she had no trouble carrying them. Going downstairs, she and her son left the hotel without encountering any of its employees. Nor, as they were making their way by the light of a three-quarters' moon, did they see any other human beings. Arriving at the livery barn, they found it too was deserted. However, while the owner had already removed all his stock and transportable property, their three fine horses were still in the stalls and their vehicle was beneath the lean-to outside the building.

Removing the low horned, double girthed range saddle, Jessica helped load the trunk and two portmanteaus on to the flat boot at the rear of the elegant Rockaway road coach. While her son was fetching out the horses, she covered and secured it with its tarpaulin. Placing the saddle inside the vehicle, she took the horse upon which it would have been used and fastened the lead rope of the head-stall to a bracket at the rear. Lending a hand to hitch the team, the speed at which she and her son made ready for departure showed this was not the first time they had been compelled by circumstances to do so without other help.

'I'll ride on the box with you for the time being,' the woman announced, as she normally travelled inside the vehicle either with her son or alone if Kinsella was not accompanying them.

'Yes, momma,' Front de Boeuf assented, guessing why the decision had been made. 'They may ha—!'

'I knowed I'd find you here!' a voice snarled.

Looking over his shoulder, as he was about to help his mother on to the driver's box, the young man saw the elderly deputy approaching. Despite weaving a little on his feet and speaking with a slurred tone suggesting he had not yet fully thrown off the effect of the blow he had received, the peace officer was holding a cut down shotgun from the rack in the office with disconcerting steadiness. Nor, as Front de Boeuf started to swing slowly around, did he act in a way which implied he might still be too dazed and bewildered to use it.

'Stay put and keep both hands where I can see 'em, you smart-assed, tinhorn son-of-a-bitch!' the deputy commanded, gesturing in unmistakable menace with the shotgun. 'You make even just one teensy god-damned wrong move and I'll not be needing to *walk* you back to the jailhouse!'

'And what might be wrong, my good man?' Jessica demanded, her manner imperious.

'*Wrong*?' the peace officer barked, impressed by the demeanour of the beautiful and statuesque woman in spite of his anger. Then his feelings reasserted themselves and he continued heatedly, 'I'll tell you what the "mother-something"[3] hell's wr—!'

'Refrain from using such *foul* language in my presence, if you please!' Jessica interrupted, ignoring the fact that she could—and on occasion did—put tongue to a flow of profanity more suitable to a thirty-year cavalry top sergeant. 'I'm not used to listening to it.'

'I'll tell you what the—what's *wrong*, ma'am!' the deputy

3. See Paragraph Three of our AUTHOR'S NOTE. J.T.E.

30

modified instinctively, having had experience of how much trouble a wealthy woman could cause if aroused. 'That son of your'n come close to caving in my head when he bust out of jail!'

'We're both aware that he had a perfectly sound reason for wishing to leave,' Jessica stated, moving a few steps away from her son. 'But how did he manage to overcome a man with your *vast* experience?'

'He told me's how he'd—!' the peace officer began.

'Yes?' the woman prompted, when the explanation was not completed.

'H—H—H—!' the deputy spluttered, trying to think of some way of putting his motives in a satisfactory light.

'I offered to pay him a fine to let me leave, momma,' Front de Boeuf put in, sounding more like a petulant and guilty child than a grown and powerful man.

'And, instead of paying this poor fellow,' Jessica guessed, her tone suggesting repugnance. 'You attacked him when he opened the door.'

'W—Well, yes, momma,' the massive young man confessed, looking sheepish.

'In that case,' the beautiful woman sighed, dipping her right hand into the neck of the reticule she was still carrying in the left. 'As usual, it is left to me to settle what amounts to a debt of honour you have incurred!'

'If you please, momma,' Front de Boeuf requested, holding both arms out well clear of his sides.

'Very well,' Jessica assented and, as she brought the right hand back into view, her voice took on a harder timbre. 'Lower that shotgun!'

'Wh—?' the deputy gasped, looking into the superposed twin barrels of the nickel plated Remington Double Derringer which the woman had produced from the reticule.

'You heard me!' Jessica hissed, thumb-cocking the hammer.

'S—Sure, ma'am!' the peace officer admitted, frightened by the cold and deadly way in which he was being addressed. Realizing he had fallen into a trap which no man could have

31

sprung upon him, he could not see any way of avenging himself against the escaped prisoner except at the cost of his own life. Convinced the beautiful woman was not bluffing, he removed his forefinger from the twin triggers and lowered the shotgun. 'Take it easy, lady, I only—!'

Waiting until the weapon was no longer posing a threat to the life of her son, Jessica tightened her right forefinger. A spurt of flame erupted from the upper barrel of the small pistol. Taken in the centre of the forehead by the .41 calibre bullet, the elderly peace officer dropped the shotgun and, pitching over backwards, fell lifeless to the ground.

'We couldn't have left him alive to come after us later,' the woman remarked, showing no concern over having taken the life of another human being and one, moreover, who was an officer in a law enforcement agency. 'Which, unless I was *very* wrong about him, he would have.'

'Yes, momma,' Front de Boueuf agreed, displaying just as little regret.

'Let's be on our way,' Jessica ordered, returning the smoking Derringer to her reticule. 'When his body is found, everybody will blame the Cousins' gang.'

'The marshal might not,' the young man warned.

'Perhaps not,' the woman replied. 'Although, judging by his conversation and behaviour, he hasn't the brains of a louse. Anyway, he's the one who the gang are coming after and, with any luck, they'll get rid of him for us. Listen, isn't that riders coming?'

'From the other side of town,' Front de Boeuf estimated, having done as he was instructed. 'But I can't hear anything in the direction we'll be going.'

'Or me,' Jessica seconded. 'So we should be safe going that way. Come along. It's high time we were leaving!'

CHAPTER THREE

They Could Kill Cousin Mark

'Looks like the boss wasn't just being ornery when he said for us to come and wait out here, Jacko,' declared the tallest of the three men in cowhand style clothing, carrying the Winchester Model of 1866 rifles. They had emerged on foot from amongst the bushes and now stood blocking the trail. 'Here's two's didn't stick around until the boys got in and've run this way.'

'Sure thing, Slim,' agreed the shortest, studying the occupants of the Rockaway road coach by the light of the moon and the carriage lights. The coach was approaching the place in the woodland allocated to himself and his companions by the leader of their gang. 'Fancy dressed couple in a real classy rig like this ought to be's good pickings as the rest of the boys'll come by in that one-hoss town.'

Until being confronted by the trio, Jessica and Trudeau Front de Bouef had had the trail they were driving along to themselves. If anybody else from Benson City had taken flight to escape the vengeance of Frank Cousins and his outlaws, some other escape route was being used. For all that, the unscrupulous couple had felt sure their departure was a wise precaution. Shots had begun to crash out from within the limits of the small town shortly after they had left and could still be heard, although there was no suggestion of pursuit, over the mile or so they had covered.

The massive young man had not spoken to his mother as he was keeping the two spirited horses drawing the coach

33

moving at a fast trot. However, his silence was not caused by either revulsion or disapproval over the murder of the elderly deputy town marshal. He had, in fact, expected something of the sort when she had ordered the peace officer to lower the shotgun. It was not the first time, although never so blatantly, that she had taken the life of another human being to help them evade the consequences of a crime. She might have acted in a less lethal fashion under different circumstances, but expediency rather than any moral considerations would have been her motive as she was completely lacking in scruples.

Thinking about the reason for their hurried departure, as he was guiding the coach away from the livery barn, something had occurred to Front de Boeuf. Wanting to consider how his idea might be put into effect before discussing it with her, he had not attempted to start a conversation of any kind. Knowing him well, the statuesque and beautiful black haired woman had not interrupted his reverie. For all her apparent disdain concerning his intelligence and ability to look after himself, which stemmed from a resentment that his presence was a constant reminder to one and all that she was no longer in the first flush of youth, she acknowledged to herself that he was both shrewd and competent. Therefore, no matter what might be causing his silence, she considered the end result would at least offer a possibility of being profitable to them.

At the conclusion of his thoughts, Front de Boeuf glanced behind and saw a red glow which suggested some of the buildings in the town had been set on fire by the outlaws. Front de Boeuf was on the point of telling his mother of the scheme he was considering when the three men waiting on the trail put in their appearance.

Although they had not lit their carriage lamps before setting out from Benson City or on the more open terrain behind them, on arriving at the area of woodland through which they were now travelling, the Front de Boeufs had decided it could prove unwise to continue without illumination. The trail was far from smooth and level. It had numerous potholes which could cause injury to a horse

34

stepping, or damage a wheel dropping, into one. To lessen the chance of this happening, they had lit the wicks of the lamps fitted to each side of the box. The light allowed them to see the men clearly, but they were aware that it also allowed them to be seen with an equal clarity.

'Don't do nothing smart-assed, fat feller!' warned the tallest of the outlaws, making a threatening motion with the rifle. 'Just stop that rig real careful and climb down with both hands showing all the time!'

'Y—Yes, sir!' Front de Boeuf answered, with the suggestion of quavering alarm he was so good at adopting when circumstances required. Although his mother and he were acquainted with some of the Cousins' gang, he could not recognize any of the trio. Nor did he think they would be swayed from their purpose by a claim to be friendly with their leader. Having also concluded resistance would be futile, at least for the time being, he decided that acting in such a fashion was the best course for him to follow. 'D— Don't sh —shoot, pl—please!'

While speaking, the massive young man conveyed the impression of being in such a state of agitation that he was inadvertently turning the team away from the trio. Before any of them could object, he brought the vehicle to a halt at an angle across the trail and with his bulky body between his mother and them. A glance her way elicited a surreptitious nod of approval. Despite being unable to discuss how they might be able to deal with the situation, each was confident the other would deduce what was wanted and act accordingly.

Looping together the reins, which passed through slots on either side at the top of the driving box's perpendicular footboard, Front de Boeuf dropped them. Then, moving slowly as if in such poor physical condition he was finding the activity a considerable exertion, he lowered himself to the ground. Having done so, keeping both hands well away from his sides—as he had when confronted by the elderly deputy town marshal outside the livery barn—but also contriving to prevent his weapons from being seen, he reached beneath the seat.

'I—I'm only g—getting this w—weight thing out, g—gentlemen!' the young man explained querulously, or so it seemed to the three outlaws, positioning himself so they could see he was not producing a firearm of any kind. 'Th—There isn't a b—brake, except for it, so I want to make sure the horses don't run away while momma is still on the coach!'

Displaying the short piece of rope, with a heavy wrought iron weight on one end and a spring clip at the other, Front de Boeuf behaved as though lifting it was a much greater strain than actually was the case. Carrying it forward, with an appearance of hesitancy, as if expecting to be attacked at any moment, he attached the clip to the metal ring on the tip of the harness pole separating the horses. Having fitted the device, a standard item serving as a brake for such vehicles, he stepped back to halt level with the rump of the nearer animal and stood with his flat palms showing to the outlaws.

'Well I swan!' commented the member of the trio who had so far remained silent, although anybody who knew Front de Boeuf well would have found his submissive behaviour most suspicious. 'He ain't the *bravest* son of a bitch I've come across, but he's close to being smart!'

'There's no gainsaying *that*, Jacko!' Slim conceded and turned his attention to the woman on the coach. 'Haul your ass down offen there, missus!'

'Very well,' Jessica assented, although in different circumstances to have been addressed in such a fashion would have produced a display of imperious anger.

Picking up her reticule, feeling thankful that she had replaced the spent cartridge in the Remington Double Derringer as soon as the vehicle was on the move, the woman slid across the box. Normally, if her son had not been there to supply it, she would have demanded assistance to descend from the nearest man. On this occasion, she began to climb from the box unaided. As she was doing so, she contrived to

36

hook the hem of her skirt over the handle of the door giving access to the body of the vehicle.

Provided somewhat more generously with material than was fashionable, the garment was able to hitch upwards without any great hindrance to the movements of its wearer. It did, however, produce one effect which might have been considered less than desirable in most circumstances. The carriage lamps were positioned to supply illumination for disembarking, or boarding, passengers, as well as the trail ahead. Therefore, on reaching the ground without attempting to make any adjustment to her attire, more than just her high buttoned shoes were exposed to view in the light.

Noticing the pair of shapely legs in black silk stockings which were being displayed, to a height well above the limit of the kind of drawers which would have been worn by a 'good' woman, the attention of the three outlaws was diverted. Already lulled into a condition of overconfidence by the slothful and seemingly frightened behaviour of her son, the sight Jessica was presenting as she was descending served to obliterate whatever lingering thoughts of caution might have remained.

Soon the lower limbs were being exhibited to a level which displayed frilly scarlet garters around the stockings and which suggested the woman either wore far more brief and daring nether garments than was implied by her appearance of respectability, or that she considered them totally unnecessary. Finding the prospect intriguing, no matter which might prove the case, the outlaws were much less watchful than they would have been in other circumstances. Instead of keeping the massive young man under constant surveillance, they were giving all their attention to his mother in the hope of discovering if she was in fact wearing underclothing of any kind.

As had happened when he was faced by the elderly deputy, and on other occasions, Front de Boeuf had expected Jessica to do something which would help them out of their predicament. It was for this reason he had brought the coach to a halt in such a fashion. At first, he had thought she might take advantage of being hidden behind his bulky body by drawing the twin barrelled pistol from her reticule. As she had not, clearly having considered to do so would entail too much of a risk, he had collected the hitching weight and secured the horses. With this done, he had taken up a position to await whatever action she decided upon. Unlike the trio, he knew the catching of the skirt on the handle of the door was no accident and he was ready to make the most of the opportunity it was creating.

Waiting until the outlaws were all engrossed in looking at his mother, the massive young man reached across with his right hand and closed it around the ivory butt of the Colt Pocket Pistol of Navy calibre. While the twin barrelled, ten gauge, whipit gun would have been far more potent, he had concluded the revolver was better suited to his needs at that moment. Not only did it offer five shots, as opposed to the two shells carried in the Greener, but the sound of its discharge was less likely to reach the town and warn the rest of the gang that the men sent to prevent such departures were in difficulties. Furthermore, a single bullet would be less dangerous to his mother than a spreading cloud of buckshot balls.

Slipping the Colt from the carefully designed slit in his fancy vest, Front de Boeuf brought his left hand to join the right as it emerged. Thumb cocking the action, he raised the weapon to shoulder height and at arms' length. This allowed him to take a better aim than would have been possible by using instinctive alignment from waist level. Aware that the combination of a comparatively small powder charge, light calibre and short barrel did not provide the shock on impact of a heavier firearm, he knew accuracy would be required to ensure an instantaneous kill. With that in mind, aware it alone would serve their purpose, he took the slightly longer time he needed to be certain of the first bullet he discharged striking the nearest of the outlaws in the head.

Having fired, as was required by the single action mechanism, the massive young man was drawing back the hammer once more with his thumbs while turning the four inch barrel.

He squeezed the trigger with his right forefinger as Jacko, alerted to the danger by the stricken outlaw spinning around and tossing aside the Winchester Model of 1866 rifle, started to turn upon him. Sending off the second shot, even as flame was spurting from the muzzle, he knew he could not act swiftly enough to prevent the last of the trio shooting at him.

At that moment, as had been the case more than once in the past, Front de Boeuf was aware that his continued existence was dependant upon the completely immoral and domineering black haired beauty who had given birth to him!

Nor was the young man let down in his latest moment of dire need!

'Scum!'

As he was swinging around his rifle to meet the danger created by the massive young man whom he and his companions had dismissed as a spineless coward, Slim heard the word spoken with such savage contempt by Jessica and glanced her way. What he saw caused him to pause for a moment. However, he was not granted any opportunity to consider what to do for the best.

Having removed the Remington from the reticule as soon as her son opened fire upon the first outlaw, the beautiful woman showed no more compunction than when shooting the elderly deputy in Benson City. Even as Jacko received the second bullet from the Colt, she discharged both barrels from the little pistol in rapid succession. Fired to prevent any chance of reprisals, as those from her son's weapons had been, the conical pieces of lead ripped into the head of the remaining outlaw. Twirling involuntarily and discarding his Winchester, he joined his two already lifeless companions on the ground. He was just as dead when he arrived.

Seeing he had no further need to concern himself with the outlaws, Front de Boeuf discarded his somnolent posture and sprang rapidly to the heads of the horses. Thrusting away his Colt, he caught hold of their reins. Despite their high spirits, being well trained and gun steady, they had not been put into a state of panic by the shots and he had no difficulty in restraining them.

'I don't hear anybody coming,' Jessica remarked, freeing and allowing the hem of the skirt to fall into its more conventional position.

'Or me,' the young man seconded, returning the Colt to its slot in his vest. 'But I don't think we should leave these three to be found, momma. Do you?'

'Of course not,' the woman confirmed, putting away the Remington. 'Go and find their horses while I search them and put their weapons in the coach. I'm sure we can find a buyer for them somewhere along the way.'

'Yes, momma,' Front de Boeuf agreed and set off to carry out his orders.

* * *

'Well, Trudeau,' Jessica Front de Boeuf said, shortly after the interrupted journey was resumed. 'And what is it you have been thinking about so deeply since we left Benson City?'

By the time the massive young man had returned, leading the horses belonging to the three dead outlaws, his mother was just completing her part in the preparations for departure. Showing no revulsion over the unsavoury task, she had gone through the pockets of the corpses and transferred the valuables she found to her reticule. Then she had removed the gunbelts, placing them and the Winchester rifles inside the coach to be sold in some small town where no questions would be asked.

Loading and fastening the bodies across the saddles, the woman and her son had chased the animals into the woodland. To further reduce the chance of Frank Cousins suspecting something other than desertion was responsible for the trio being missing, knowing the burdened horses were likely to keep going for a considerable distance and might even return to wherever was regarded as home, they had contrived to cover the bloodstains on the trail before leaving.

'Thinking about?' Trudeau Front de Bouef replied and a

slightly defensive note came into his voice. 'Why, Aunt Cornelia's will!'

'*Aunt Cornelia's will*?' the beautiful woman repeated, her tone indicating she found the subject far from pleasant.

'Yes, momma,' the young man confirmed, his manner becoming somewhat defiant although he kept his gaze to the front. '*Aunt Cornelia's will*!'

'And what about Aunt Cornelia's will?'

'She's said she meant to change it and leave *everything* to Cousin Mark.'

'I know *that*!' Jessica hissed in tones of righteous indignation. 'And, even though Lawyer Sneiton hasn't let us know it's already been done, there's nothing more sure than that she will do it, the vindictive old bitch!'

'As you say, momma, she will do it and in all probability has already,' Front de Boeuf drawled. However, he was too tactful to point out that it was the fault of his parent that they had been threatened with being cut out of the legacy they were discussing. She had stolen money from and forged the name of the aunt in question on a cheque to obtain a piece of jewellery which had taken her fancy. 'But, to be the beneficiary, Cousin Mark will have to outlive her.'

'Of course he will, that's *obvious*!' the woman snorted, yet there was far more speculation than disdain in the glance she turned towards her massive offspring. 'And, as he is two years younger than you and she's in her late sixties, I would imagine the odds of outliving her are greatly in his favour.'

'That's true under natural conditions, momma,' the young man admitted. 'But Cousin Mark doesn't lead anywhere nearly such a sheltered life as Aunt Cornelia.'

'Who does?' Jessica complained bitterly, ignoring the fact that her dishonesty and promiscuity had been responsible for her own far from leisurely life-style. 'However, despite all I've heard about what he's been up to since he came back from serving with Bushrod Sheldon in Mexico after the War, I'd rather not have to rely upon him getting killed before that old battle-axe finally gets around to dying.'

'Or I, momma,' Front de Boeuf supported. 'At least, not if

we just wait for it to happen. Of course, he could be helped on his way.'

'Helped,' Jessica queried, having devoted considerable thought to the possibility ever since Cornelia Front de Boeuf had announced her intention of making Mark Counter—a nephew born and residing in Texas—sole beneficiary to her sizeable fortune. After having spent a few seconds trying to decide what her son had in mind, she went on, 'You mean if he should be killed by somebody?'

'Yes, momma,' the young man confirmed, taking pleasure from for once being able to confuse his mother. 'If he should be killed by *somebody* is just what I mean.'

'Huh!' the woman sniffed. 'I haven't just sat around waiting for Sneiton to let us know she's changed her will. Ever since I heard what she meant to do, I've been sounding out men to get rid of him. But none of them were willing to take the chance, no matter what I offered them. Not only is young Counter considered to be very good with a gun on his own account, but he rides with Captain Fog in something they call, "Ole Devil's floating outfit" and that seems to scare the shit out of everybody I've asked.'

'I'm not surprised, momma,' Front de Boeuf asserted, having heard many stories about the fighting abilities of Captain Dustine Edward Marsden 'Dusty' Fog and the men who formed the elite floating outfit of the OD Connected ranch owned by General Jackson Baines "Ole Devil" Hardin. 'Only I wasn't thinking of getting some hired gun to go up against Cousin Mark. If he was caught, instead of being killed outright, that part Comanche they call the Ysabel Kid would make him tell who had hired him and we don't want *that* to happen.'

'We *don't*, they wouldn't be as lenient as Aunt Cornelia,' Jessica said vehemently, her knowledge of Ole Devil's floating outfit being much more extensive than she had pretended. Then she swung on the seat to stare at her son in genuine alarm and continued, 'Great merciful heavens, Tru. You aren't thinking of going up against him yourself?'

'No, momma,' Front de Boeuf stated reassuringly, re-

42

membering that as children Mark Counter had always been the only member of their group who could best him in a fight or other test of strength and ready to believe all he had heard about the prowess his cousin had acquired as a lightning fast and deadly gun fighter.[1] 'I've never even *thought* of going up against himself myself.'

'Then who's to do it?'

'Frank Cousins.'

'Frank Cousins?'

'Yes, momma. He and his men could kill Cousin Mark in a way which would prevent the slightest suspicion falling upon us.'

'But, particularly with the way things are going down here in Texas at the moment, why would Frank Cousins go after him?'

'You know what they say about the Cousins' clan, momma,' the young man replied. 'If you cut one, they all bleed. That's why they're raiding Benson City tonight.'

'I know why they're doing it,' the woman pointed out, but she had not resumed her disdainful manner despite the objections she started to express. 'No, Tru. Even if we could arrange for young Counter to kill one or more of the family, I can't see Frank Cousins finding men willing to go with him to raid Ole Devil Hardin's ranch. I've told you how the hired guns I've approached behave when I told them I wanted him killing.'

'Yes, momma, you've told me,' Front de Boeuf answered. 'But I wasn't thinking of having a Cousins killed by Cousin Mark. It isn't only the Cousins' clan who all bleed if you cut one.'

1. Details of the career and special qualifications of Mark Counter, plus some information regarding General Jackson Baines 'Ole Devil' Hardin, C.S.A., Captain Dustine Edward Marsden 'Dusty' Fog, C.S.A. and the Ysabel Kid can be found in: APPENDIX ONE. J.T.E.

CHAPTER FOUR

A Bad Loser

'All right, god damn it!' ejaculated the best dressed of the five young men engaged in a poker game for moderate stakes at the Davey Crockett Saloon in San Antonio de Bexar. His Kansas accent indicated extreme impatience as he continued, 'I'll call. Let's see what you have!'

Tall, slim, black haired and sullenly handsome, the speaker was in his early twenties. Like three more of the players, he was wearing the attire of a cowhand. However, he was more of a dandy than they were, albeit one of limited means. There were conchas on the rattlesnake skin band of the black hat—its crown a 'Montana peak' in defiance of the fashion in Texas—dangling by its *barbiquejo* chinstrap from the back of his chair. They were, in fact, of a baser metal than the silver they pretended to be. His glossy dark blue shirt and black trousers were not made from the best quality materials. Despite the fact that the general tone of his garments suggested how he might earn his living, his boots had low heels more suited to walking than riding. He had on a gunbelt, with an ivory handled Colt 1860 Army Model revolver in its fast draw holster, but to experienced eyes this did not have the look of having originated from a top grade leatherworker.

In addition to regarding himself as the favourite nephew of Frank Cousins, by virtue of his father being an attorney-at-law well versed in court procedure and every loophole in the legal system, the young man always thought of himself as a

44

poker player of great skill. Therefore, particularly when he considered who was doing most of the winning in the present game, he felt his luck had been out since the game commenced, and he was never one to suffer adversity with good grace. In fact, as the other three participants who knew him were aware, he was always a bad loser.

Taking into consideration the way in which the current round of betting had gone, Brock Cousins concluded that —despite having declined to take even one card when offered the opportunity by the dealer—the remaining player in the pot was holding a hand of similar value to his own. The point about which he felt less sure was whether it was of a lower rank.[1] Although he had seen one ace amongst the discards and knew that the higher of his two pairs were kings, he was disinclined to back his assessment to the extent of raising the bet when he recollected how misfortune had dogged him all evening. Instead, he had opted for a safer alternative. It was one which, no matter what the result of the call, would still leave him with sufficient cash to continue playing and, hopefully, at least recoup some of his losses.

'See 'em, huh?' inquired the player who had been called, speaking after the manner of a poorly educated Southron and, although his behaviour did not indicate this to be the case, one whose wits were somewhat slow.

'Yeah!' the dandy answered. 'Show me what you've got!'

'Two pairs is all,' the challenged player declared, turning over the queens of hearts and clubs.

'Got you this time, by God!' Cousins enthused, without waiting to hear or see any more. Displaying two kings, two fives and a seven, he reached eagerly for the money in the centre of the table as he went on, 'And about ti—!'

'Hold on a cotton-picking minute, I wouldn't come right on out 'n' say that's your'n at all,' the other player drawled, flipping over the rest of his cards to show they were two aces and a nine.

1. *An explanation of the types of 'hands' in the game of poker and their respective values is given in:* TWO MILES TO THE BORDER. *J.T.E.*

45

'B—But you said—!' the dandy spluttered in indignation.

'All I said was I had two pairs,' the player interrupted. 'And, being raised right 'n' proper, I figured it was only polite-like for the ladies to go first and showed 'em afore these here two lil ole bullets's've killed those kings of your'n stone dead. But I didn't *never* at no time allow's my two pairs was only queen high.'

'And that's the truth, Grizzly B'ar!' Albert "Albie" Tuttle put in hurriedly, seeing anger was darkening the face of the loser. Of medium height, strongly built, brown haired and, as a general rule, of cheerful countenance, at twenty-six he was the oldest of the quartet belonging to the gang of Frank Cousins. Although not always prone to behaving in such a responsible fashion, he remembered the orders they had been given regarding their conduct while visiting San Antonio and he wanted to avoid trouble. 'Seeing's how two aces beats two kings, no matter whether they was *shown* first or last, you've won again, Grizzly. Ain't he, Brock?'

'Yeah, I reckon he has,' Cousins conceded, his manner grudging, after a glance at his other two companions had warned him that they too were remembering what they had been told by his uncle. There was something else that persuaded him to yield reasonably quietly. While he considered himself to be tough and fast on the draw, in addition to being a skilful poker player, he was conscious of the fact that his revolver was still in its holster and his opponent's was not. Therefore, he merely removed his hands from the money and kept them in plain view as he went on, showing no better grace, 'You're real *lucky*, Grizzly Bear, I'll give you *that*!'

'Now I get real *pleasured* from hearing's how you'll "*give*" me that much,' Trudeau Front de Boeuf asserted, his tone harsh and more uncouth in timbre than was usual, having supplied the alias, "Grizzly Bear", when joining the game. His massive right hand, its pallid softness rendered less obvious by having been deliberately made dirty, tapped the table close to the walnut butt of the Army Colt he had placed in front of him when he sat down and he continued just as menacingly, ' 'Cepting it's better'n playing with any

46

kind of *winner*, I surely hate to play with a bad loser. But leave us not forget's how it was *you* who shuffled the son-of-bitching deck, Brock, 'n' good ole Burro there cut the bastard afore *you* dealt. All I did was sit here and play the cards's *you* give to me.'

'Hey now, don't get riled, big feller!' Cousins requested with alacrity. Despite hating to have to adopt such a conciliatory line, when he looked at a much more readily accessible weapon than his own, he was forced to sound more amiable than he was feeling. 'I didn't say's there was anything *wrong* with you winning *again*. I just wish I was as lucky as you've been since you sat in with us.'

Under the circumstances, there was good cuase for the apology!

In spite of having his three companions present, the young dandy considered he would be ill-advised to antagonize the massive player he was addressing. He suspected that, even if nothing worse happened to him personally as a result of his having caused trouble, to do so would provoke the kind of situation he and his cronies had been told to avoid. Certainly 'Grizzly Bear' did not strike him as likely to be unduly perturbed by knowing to whom he was closely related and, while he was sure his uncle—mindful of the reputation upon which the safety of the family depended—would make every effort to avenge him, it would be no comfort to him after he was dead. Nothing he had seen of 'Grizzly Bear's' behaviour during their short acquaintance suggested he would have any hesitation in meeting aggression with violence if he were aroused or crossed.

For once, Trudeau Front de Boeuf was not exuding his usual suggestion of pampered softness which had frequently led people to form erroneous conclusions about his nature!

In fact, particularly at that moment, he was giving exactly the opposite effect!

Glowering across the table, the massive young man was contriving to look as savage and dangerous as a grizzly bear freshly wakened from its winter sleep and 'on the prod' because it was starving!

47

The long and greasy black 'hair' of a wig was straggling from beneath the battered old hat, so coated with dust as to render its original colour practically indistinguishable. What small portion of his face was not obscured by a realistic false beard had been stained dark brown and was as grimy as his hands. He had on a loose fitting and grubby brown coat. His collarless shirt, with his throat hidden by a filthy and indistinctly coloured bandana, had changed from white to a murky grey. Just as dirty yellowish-brown Nankeen trousers were tucked into the much-scuffed legs of low-heeled, blunt toed, unpolished boots. Strapped about his middle was a gunbelt which was made up by the storekeeper who had purchased all but one of the rifles and a revolver taken from the three dead outlaws on the trail out of Benson City. It had a cross draw holster for the retained Army Colt at the right side. Although he had allowed the other players to see he was carrying the Greener whipit gun in its usual fashion, the Colt Pocket Pistol of Navy Calibre was hidden behind his back in the waist band of his trousers.

While Jessica Front de Boeuf had agreed that the plan for bringing about the death of Mark Counter was worth trying, she had insisted they waited until they discovered how they would be affected by what had happened in Benson City. However, Front de Boeuf was not wearing his disguise as a result of their activities immediately prior to leaving the town.

Hearing that the death of the elderly deputy had been attributed to the Cousins' gang, who had shot the town marshal as he was leaving the Central Hotel, the unscrupulous woman had responded shrewdly. Sending a letter to the judge, she had given an explanation of why the body of her son had not been found in the burned out remains of the jailhouse. Enclosing fifty of the dollars they had looted from the outlaws they killed, she had explained these were for the dependants of the 'good-hearted old peace officer who had kindly released my son so he could come and protect me when the Cousins gang raided the town!' She had also suggested that Front de Boeuf should return to complete his sentence as this would allow the judge and herself to become better acquainted. Replying to the address she had given, although neither she nor her son were there and the answer was delivered to them by an effective system they had established, he returned the money on the grounds that the deputy had no dependants. He had concluded that he too hoped they might meet again, but considered there was no need for her and her offspring to return at the moment. Having contrived to arouse the jealousy of his wife during the trial, as part of the scheme to ensure Front de Boeuf would be given a jail sentence thereby supplying them with a reason for remaining in town, she had expected some such response when making her suggestion.

Satisfied they would not be sought by the law, the mother and son had ascertained that they were in no danger from another source. From what they had learned, via their numerous contacts amongst the criminal elements of Texas, neither Frank Cousins nor the rest of the gang were worried over the absence of the three outlaws they had shot. This was put down to nothing more than desertion. The trio were known to be malcontents and, it was assumed, had quit as a result of being punished by receiving a task which would have kept them from taking part in the looting of the town. If any of their bodies had been found, there was no reference to it in the newspapers or by word of mouth.

Relieved of the possibility of reprisals from that direction, and also having contacted 'Smokey' Hill Thompson—who was angry over having been deprived of the opportunity of robbing the bank in Benson City—and established they had carried out their assignment on his behalf, the Front de Boeufs had directed their energies to obtaining pertinent information regarding the members of the Cousins' clan. Fortune had favoured them. Learning that the person they considered best suited to their purpose was planning a visit to San Antonio with three companions, they had travelled there. On arriving, they had made preparations for making the acquaintance of the four young outlaws.

One of the things that had been decided was that Front de

Boeuf should adopt an appearance which would be more likely to impress and overawe the quartet than might prove the case without the disguise. It could perhaps help in another direction. Past experience had warned the couple that for him to sit in a poker game dressed after the fashion of a successful professional gambler was apt to arouse suspicions, not always unjustified, should he start winning. As it was, his new *persona* had led the quartet to consider him more in the light of a potential victim—albeit perhaps a risky one—when he had asked if he could join them.

All four, especially Cousins, had soon learned the error of their assumption!

A most experienced poker player, with a thorough knowledge of most other types of gambling games, Front de Boeuf was equally competent whether depending upon fair means or foul. It had soon become obvious to him that he would have no need to cheat against opposition of such a poor quality. Therefore, instead of employing any of the cheating methods he knew would ensure things went in his favour, he had subjected the quartet to the tactics employed by a honest 'wolf' when in the company of those he concluded were belonging to the category known as possessing the 'Sign of the Rabbit'.

During the play, the massive young man had allowed his opponents to 'buy' cheap straights and flushes. He had half bluffed when he was dealt a strong hand, calling as if considering it was only of medium value. Or, if nobody called him, he would toss the cards down undisplayed and imply that they had foolishly allowed him to win with a 'seven-high-nothing'. This had led to one or another victim swearing to call him next time, if only to keep him 'honest' and, on losing, they would be informed disdainfully that he was holding a much stronger hand than the other's.

These were not the only subterfuges from the border line of poker ethics which Front de Boeuf had brought from his bag of tricks. He would make a 'mouth bet', but apply an irritant by declining—as he could do legitimately—to back it up by putting the sum he quoted into the pot. On being

50

called, should he have said he was holding 'threes', his opponent had to wait to find out whether he meant a pair of threes or three of a kind. He was aware that, as he had done with Cousins, few things had a more distracting effect than to be allowed to believe one had won a pot and then learn this was not the case. Between the pots, he had boasted of his prowess with members of the opposite sex, recounted his successes in other fields of endeavour and spoken of coups he had pulled in other games.

Such tactics had served to have an adverse effect upon the judgement of the four young outlaws!

There were others, just as effective!

As the game was for 'table stakes',[2] on winning a pot —knowing nothing riled up an impatient player such as Cousins had proved to be, especially when losing, than the practice of 'ratholing'—Front de Boeuf would pocket a proportion of the money he drew in and, in accordance with the rules, would bet with what he had before him. On one occasion, he had contrived to burn the fingers of tallish, lanky, Wilfred 'Burro' Dankey with the cigar he was smoking and had apologized, blaming the mishap upon the excessive amount of cash lying in front of him. Deciding he was up against a 'tight' player, from the way in which middle-sized and thickset Barry Sims piled coins into easily evaluated stacks, this was the direction in which he had shot most of his bluffs. Such a mentality was disinclined to take chances and was more ready than a reckless player to discard a hand when faced with a large raise in the betting. While a somewhat better player than the other three, Tuttle had also suffered at his hands.

With the passing of time, Front de Boeuf had taken much of the quartet's money. He had also studied them and formed an accurate assessment of their characters and combined with something his mother had overheard them discussing

---

2. 'Table stakes': an agreed limit, generally restricting each player to whatever money he or she has on the table at the beginning, arrived at before the game is started. J.T.E.

earlier in the day, he began to feel confident that he would be able to persuade them to do what was necessary for his scheme. Fortunately, his belligerent demeanour and imposing bulk, aided by the orders which they had received regarding their behaviour in town had proved sufficient to prevent any of them from openly, or actively, resenting their repeated losses to him.

Wanting to try and recover some of the money taken by the 'hairy' giant, Dankey was gathering up the cards while the conversation was taking place. As was the case with his companions, he did not notice three men who had come into the bar-room. Nor, with one exception, did anybody else present pay the slightest attention to the newcomers. Despite being named after one of Texas's most revered heroes, it was unwise to display curiosity in the Davey Crockett Saloon.

Wearing range clothes no better nor worse than those of the majority of the other customers, tall, gaunt and unshaven, the trio were carrying revolvers in low hanging fast draw holsters. There was a wary and watchful air about them, but this was typical of the kind of clientele attracted by the establishment as it was in the least salubrious section of the city. Glancing around, clearly in search of somebody, their examination came to a halt on reaching the table at which the poker game was taking place. Then they started to walk forward in a loose arrowhead formation. Coming to a halt, still without any of the young outlaws showing signs of being aware they had arrived, each of them drew and cocked his revolver.

'Albie Tuttle?' asked the oldest and central of the trio.

'That's me,' admitted the outlaw in question, looking around. Finding himself staring into the muzzle of a cocked Army Colt, he stiffened in alarm and gasped, 'What the h—?'

'We're wanting you 'n' Burro Dankey there,' the spokesman for the trio announced in a harsh voice, while his companions were keeping a careful watch upon most of the quintet seated around the table. 'Dodgers on you both say, "Dead Or Alive", which it don't make no never mi—!'

'*Dodgers*?' Tuttle gasped, aware that the wanted posters

52

put out by law enforcement agencies invariably stipulated the conditions under which the reward would be paid. 'Hell's fires, mister, you've got it all wrong. There ain't no bounty on me any place. Nor on Burro neither, comes to that!'

'There for sure ain't!' seconded Dankey, allowing the cards he had gathered to fall unheeded from his grasp. Realizing how such an action might be misconstrued, he hurriedly spread open his hands to emphasize that he had no hostile intentions and continued, 'Which, if anybody says there is, they're god-damned liars. Aren't they, Brock?'

The two young men were speaking the truth. Although they belonged to the gang run by Frank Cousins, they served in only a minor capacity. At no time had either been brought to the attention of law enforcement agencies as individuals. In fact, they were unknown to peace officers. Therefore it had come as a shock to be told wanted posters had been issued bearing their names and bounties offered for their apprehension alive or dead.

Before Cousins could say a word in defence of his companions, a frown creased the leathery face of the spokesman. Swinging his gaze, but not his revolver, towards Front de Boeuf, he began, 'Y—!'

CHAPTER FIVE

Good Pickings In Tennyson

Like so many of their kind, Brock Cousins and the three companions he had brought to San Antonio de Bexar wanted to acquire the reputation for being top grade gun fighters. To this end, they had devoted considerable time and energy in developing their ability to draw fast and shoot with reasonable accuracy. However, as yet, none of them had ever needed to put his skill to the test in mortal combat and there was much they still had need to learn.

If the quartet had been more experienced and less perturbed by the behaviour of the three men confronting them, they might have found something strange in what was taking place!

For one thing, only the four outlaws were being covered!

Despite his aura of menace and his weapon being more easily available than those of the other players, no revolver was being directed at 'Grizzly Bear'!

Nor had the unshaven trio of bounty hunters raised even a vocal objection when the massive, unprepossessing young giant had laid his right hand on the walnut butt of the Colt 1860 Army Model revolver in front of him!

In fact, until the spokesman began to address 'Grizzly Bear', none of the newcomers had paid any attention whatsoever to the disguised Trudeau Front de Boeuf. Yet their behaviour in every other respect had suggested they were all sufficiently well versed in such matters to avoid taking unnecessary chances. Certainly they had appeared to have sufficient gun savvy to prevent them from overlooking any action which might prove potentially dangerous.

On finding he was being addressed, Front de Boeuf thrust away his chair. As he swiftly rose, he also lifted and cocked the long barrelled revolver with deft speed. Directed to bring to an end a statement which he realized must not be completed, chance rather than a deliberate alignment achieved this by causing the .44 calibre soft round lead ball to enter the open mouth of the spokesman. Not only did this prevent the bounty hunter from declaring that he and his companions had been told by the 'hairy' giant that there was a reward offered for Albert 'Albie' Tuttle and Wilfred 'Burro' Dankey, but the bullet burst out through the back of his neck and inflicted a fatal wound.

Employing his right thumb to haul back the hammer, the massive young man controlled the recoil and turned the eight inches long barrel. He was moving with a rapidity which told of considerable skill, even when handling a comparatively unfamiliar weapon. Even as the startled and not a little frightened outlaws were beginning to quit their chairs, he fired the Colt again. Killing the bounty hunter standing to the left of the already falling spokesman with his second bullet, he knew he must also ensure the third was silenced if the scheme upon which he and his mother were engaged was to be given a chance to succeed.

Regardless of having devoted much thought as to how he would behave in a situation of this kind, Cousins was as alarmed as his companions by the way in which their evening's activities had taken a turn for the worse. However, despite it being the first time he had been involved in such a crisis, he retained just sufficient presence of mind to respond in a positive fashion. Bringing out his ivory handled Army Colt with the speed acquired from long practice, he shot at the third bounty hunter tricked by the Front de Boeufs—they had been brought to the Davey Crockett Saloon by Jessica, who was wearing the garish attire of a less than 'good' woman and a blonde wig—as a means of gaining the confidence of his party. Inadvertently, he caused a wound which would not have proved fatal by itself.

Already bewildered by the way in which things were going terribly wrong, the last victim of the plotting by the unscrupulous mother and son stumbled backwards, lead in his right shoulder. Although he lost his hold on the revolver he had drawn, this did not save him. Being determined to prevent the four outlaws learning what had brought about the confrontation, the 'hairy' giant cut loose another bullet in his direction. Even as it was striking the chest of the bounty hunter, it was joined by lead from the weapons Tuttle, Dankey and Barry Sims had brought from leather. Any of the wounds inflicted would have caused a mortal injury. Together, they flung their recipient in a lifeless sprawl away from the table.

Continuing to move with alacrity, Front de Boeuf took the revolver in his left hand. While he was returning it to the cross draw holster, he twisted his torso to make the side of his coat swing open and leave clear the second of his weapons. Liberated by the removal of the Colt, his right hand flashed to the butt of the Greener whipit gun and lifted it from the carrying slot of the shoulder harness. While his left hand was reaching for the foregrip, he curled his right thumb over the twin hammers and his first and second fingers each went to rest upon a trigger. Such was the extent of his span and the power with which he could grip, he was able to cock the hammers single handedly by this means.

'Should you-all have a mind to stay healthy!' the massive and "hairy" young man bellowed, moving the Greener in an arc which encompassed the whole of the bar-room. 'I'd say you'd best keep sat and 'tend to your own doings, not our'n!'

Although there were customers present who could truthfully claim to possess a salty toughness which 'took no sass but sarsparilla', the shouted command brought a complete and immediate cessation of movement. There were several men present with sufficient skill at gun handling to have ignored the warning in the face of a revolver. However, the whipit gun was a vastly different proposition. Even if the load

56

in each chamber was not in excess of nine buckshot balls, these would spread upon leaving the muzzles. Despite being only .32 in calibre, they would be sufficiently lethal as they sprayed across the room to make interference too dangerous to be contemplated.

'Now that's some more *friendly*,' Front de Boeuf declared, watching his order being obeyed. Removing his left hand from the foregrip, without allowing the Greener to sag, he swiftly scooped all his money into the capacious pocket of his loose hanging coat. However, on Cousins showing signs of duplicating his actions, he overturned the table and snapped, 'It's time we was getting the hell out of here!'

'What the hell're you doing?' Cousins yelped indignantly, pointing to the floor. 'That's *my* money you've—!'

'Stop 'n' pick it up, be you so minded,' "Grizzly Bear" replied in an indifferent fashion. 'But I'm aiming to be long gone afore the town clown and his deputies come to find out who-alls been making blue windows in those three jaspers.'

'But you—!' the dandy began.

'Stop 'n' pick it up happen you're so minded, like I said,' Front de Boeuf interrupted. 'Only I was figuring on leaving something's'll help all these good ole boys to bear in mind's how we had to start shooting in pure self defence 'cause them three bounty hunting sons-of-bitches mistook us for owlhoots when we're not.'

'Grizzly's making real good sense, Brock!' Tuttle supported, despite what was left of his money having been sprayed upon the floor when the table was tipped over. Although he had spoken the truth when claiming there were no wanted posters issued for him, he had no desire to find himself in the hands of the town marshal, and he continued, 'Come on, we can't stay here any longer!'

* * *

'Well now,' Trudeau Front de Boeuf drawled, coming to a halt in the shadows of an alley some distance from the Davey Crockett Saloon. 'It's been tolerable enjoy-ful knowing you

57

gents. Only, now I've steered you-all this far safe 'n' sound, I reckon I'll be on my way.'

Seeing all three of his companions were in agreement with 'Grizzly Bear' over the necessity of leaving the saloon before the arrival of the local peace officers, Brock Cousins had accompanied them. Once outside, the 'hairy' giant had taken advantage of their obvious lack of purpose to continue furthering his own plans. Although he already knew they were on foot, on being told they had walked from the rooming house at which they were staying, he had admitted he was also a-foot. Then, ordering them to 'holster those guns and act all innocent-like', he had offered to let them accompany him. Giving their nominal leader no chance to speak, Tuttle, Dankey and Sims had accepted. Having no greater desire to be left alone, Cousins had yielded to the wishes of the majority. Guiding them through the back streets, Front de Boeuf had continued to move ahead until certain they were not being pursued before speaking.

'Hold hard!' Cousins growled, resenting the way in which control of the party had been wrested from him. Then, noticing the "hairy" giant was still holding the whipit gun despite having insisted he and his companions put away their revolvers, he forced himself to adopt a far less aggressive tone as he went on, 'You made us come away without our money!'

'I didn't *make* you do *nothing*!' Front de Boeuf corrected and raised the Greener until its two barrels were almost touching the chest of the protester. 'Like I told you back there in the Davey Crockett, had you been so minded, you could've stayed on 'n' picked it up!'

'That's what you said all right, Grizzly,' Tuttle confirmed, albeit a trifle petulantly. Watching the whipit gun and making sure his right hand remained well away from his holstered revolver, he continued, 'Only you might've let us get our'n as well afore you throwed the table over.'

'Well, yes, I *could* have done that,' Front de Boeuf conceded, but without any suggestion of being contrite, despite the supportive muttering of the other three young outlaws. 'Only then there wouldn't've been nothing left behind for them yahoos in the barroom to pick up, 'stead of coming after us.'

'It was *our* son-of-a-bitching money that you left!' Cousins pointed out, employing as much indignation as he dare. However, his eyes never left the weapon which was still pointing at him, and he made himself control his anger. 'You'd already picked up all of your own.'

'I for certain sure had!' the 'hairy' giant admitted calmly. ' 'Spite of the way I've got myself looking, what he started to say, that bounty hunting son-of-a-bitch must've recognized me. Only it was two of you good ole boys they was after, not me. So, pleasant's I found your company, seeing's how I wouldn't've been seen by 'em had I stayed clear of you, I sure's hell's for sinners wasn't about to leave any of my own money back there.'

'So you're on the dodge, huh?' Cousins asked, the significance of what had happened just before the shooting having escaped his notice.

'Let's just say there's them around's'd like to see me,' Front de Boeuf instructed, satisfied none of the other three had been more observant. 'And, happen you're wanting to talk some more, I know a place where we can do it a whole heap safer'n out here under the sky. Anyways, I'm not fixing to stand here jawing no more, just in case we're being looked for.'

'Hell, them bunch at the Davey Crockett wouldn't dare come after us, nor tell the town clowns anything either, happen I'd let them know who I am!' Cousins claimed, seeing his companions were showing signs of accompanying the massive, "hairy" giant. He felt, under the circumstances, a reminder of his important family connections would not come amiss and continued, 'And the john laws would have made sure they steered well clear of *me*, had they been told.'

'Finding out's how you're kin of Frank Cousins would've likely stopped them jaspers in the saloon from troubling you,' Front de Boeuf conceded, pleased with the way in which the situation was developing. 'But it wouldn't mean spit, shit, nor piss in the bucket to the marshal. He knows for sure your uncle ain't going to pull no Benson City tricks—cut one and all your family bleed notwithstanding—against a town the size of San Antone. 'Specially when he's got a whole slew of Yankee blue-belly hoss-soldiers close enough to call in for backing.'

'Ole "Grizzly's" got the rights of it, Brock,' Burro Dankey supported, without realizing he was playing into the hands of the "hairy" giant. ' 'Cause that's what the boss said when he told us to steer clear of trouble down here!'

'Happen Mr. Cousins won't get to hear about what's come off, seeing's how nobody knowed us back there,' Tuttle commented, feeling sure their leader would not approve of the incident if it was brought to his attention. 'But we'd best not stick around here.'

'Ain't nothing to keep us here, anyways,' remarked Barry Sims.

'How's about grabbing a meal and lighting a shuck out f—?' Dankey suggested, ever a good trencherman, but the words died away as he realized that neither he nor any of his companions had enough money to pay for the food.

'Happen you boys're close to the blanket 'n' hungry,' Front de Boeuf drawled, returning the Greener to its shoulder harness. 'I can stake you to a meal so long's you don't want nothing fancier than re-fried *frijoles* and *chili con carne*.'

'Hot damn!' Dankey enthused. 'There ain't nothing I like better'n re-fried beans and *chili con carne*.'

'Or any other kind of victuals,' Tuttle supplemented, equally enamoured of the prospect of obtaining a meal. 'And I'd be right obliged for it, "Grizzly". 'Cepting what I'd already dropped trying to lick you, I left all my cash back to the Davey Crockett.'

'And me,' seconded Sims. 'Hell, Brock, it looks like we'll have to go to Boerne now, but we don't have enough money between us to buy even one god-damned meal afore we head up there.'

'Then we might's well take "Grizzly" up on his offer,' Cousins declared, seeing the matter was once again being taken from his hands but hoping to convey the impression that he was still in complete command of the situation. 'Where do we go, big feller?'

'This way,' Front de Boeuf replied.

Followed by the four young outlaws, satisfied that he need not fear any attempt would be made to retrieve the money he had won from them, the 'hairy' giant took a circuitous route through a part of San Antonio inhabited by the poorest members of the white population. Their destination proved to be a small adobe cabin to which was attached a dilapidated lean-to. There was no sign of the building or its adjunct being occupied. On his opening the front door without knocking, or otherwise announcing their presence, the quartet discovered the interior was illuminated and concluded there must be some form of covering over the windows. Waving them forward, 'Grizzly Bear' allowed them to precede him into what was clearly the main section. Apart from a rickety table and several rudely made chairs, there were no other furnishings. However, on crossing the threshold, none of the outlaws paid the slightest attention to their surroundings.

Having returned to the cabin by a shorter route, after watching her son and their intended victims deal with the bounty hunters from outside the front entrance to the Davey Crockett Saloon, Jessica Front de Boeuf had had time to make ready for the arrival of the party.

Wearing only brief scarlet drawers fringed with black lace, frilly red garters and black stockings, the woman strolled from the bedroom at the rear of the building. Nothing remained of her usual aristocratic and imperious demeanour. Instead, as she was wearing a somewhat straggly blonde wig and excessive make-up, she could have passed as a prostitute, better looking than most, from a not too costly brothel. However, this did not deter Cousins and his companions. They invariably found female company in such places and, despite being somewhat older than the kind which usually came their way, her scantily clad body was sufficiently curvaceous to arouse their lust.

'Lands sakes a-mercy, "Grizzly"!' Jessica shrieked, her

61

voice as strident and coarse as the tones adopted by her son. Raising her hands, apparently in an unsuccessful attempt to conceal the naked and firm mounds of her imposing bosom, she turned and, much to the disappointment of the outlaws, left the room hurriedly, crying, 'Why didn't you let on's you'd got somebody with you?'

'God damn it, Nellie, come on back out here!' Front de Boeuf commanded, not in the least embarrassed or concerned over his mother having appeared before the four outlaws in such a state of near nudity. 'Me 'n' these here good ole boys're needing some food and *tequila* while we're making *habla* together.'

'You'll have to make do with what I've got cooked up already,' the woman stated with what appeared to be sullen defiance, returning after having donned a flimsy and torn black negligee which allowed much of her figure to be visible. 'Who-all're all these fellers?'

'This here's *Frank Cousins'* nephew,' Front de Boeuf introduced, indicating the dandy, but he was not allowed to continue.

'*Frank Cousins'* nephew, huh?' Jessica repeated, eyeing the young man in question with an apparently admiring interest that he found most satisfying, even though it might have been created as a result of his influential family connections. Raising her right hand, as if wishing to tidy her "blonde" hair, she caused the negligee to open and further exhibit her otherwise unclad torso to his lascivious gaze. 'Heavens to Betsy, "Grizzly Bear", had you told me's how you'd be bringing *quality* with you, I'd've gotten something to eat better'n re-fried beans and *chili*.'

'That'll do good enough for us,' Front de Boeuf claimed. 'Go fetch it, 'stead of just standing there showing off your apples.'

'Now that's what I call one hell of a well shaped woman,' Tuttle asserted, watching the voluptuous "blonde" disappearing with a hip-rolling gait into the second of the rooms at the rear.

'That she is!' Cousins seconded vehemently, then swung a

62

worried gaze towards the "hairy" giant. 'No offense meant, "Grizzly"!'

'And there ain't none tooken,' Front de Boeuf replied amiably. 'She's surely got all the pieces stacked right where they should be and plenty of 'em. But I tell you, fellers, she's so hot-assed there's times I get plump tuckered out just trying to keep her satisfied in bed. Anyways, haul up chairs and get sat.'

'Now that's the kind of *problem* I'd admire to have!' Tuttle declared, gazing through the open door of the kitchen to where Jessica was scooping steaming *chili con carne* on to plates from a bowl on the stove.

'And me!' Dankey seconded fervently, also admiring the view, as he and his companions collected chairs then arranged themselves around the rickety table.

'By grab, was you not headed some place urgent, I'd take you up on that,' Front de Boeuf stated. 'Only, 'less I'm mistooken, I thought I heard something said about you-all heading up to Boerne real soon.'

'Well yes,' Cousins conceded, throwing a prohibitive glare around his companions as he had no desire that the "hairy" giant should be told of the reason for the impending visit. 'We'd *thought* about going there.'

'Got them a right pretty lil ole bank in Boerne,' Front de Boeuf remarked, in what appeared to be an off-hand fashion. Hiding his amusement over the interplay of glances which passed between the quartet, his mother having contrived to overhear the reason for their interest in the town earlier in the day—wearing a red wig and clothing suitable for her pose as a saloongirl to avoid being recognized when they met later —he continued with a similar apparent lack of guile. 'Trouble with it being there ain't only me's reckons so.'

'How do you mean, "Grizzly"?' Tuttle inquired, tearing his gaze away from the open door of the kitchen and thinking how different the "hairy" giant sounded from when they had first met. While the voice was still harsh and uncouth, it had lost the suggestion of slow wittedness that it had possessed

63

when addressing the occupants of the bar-room. 'Do you know something about the bank there?'

'I could be wrong, mind,' Front de Boeuf replied, his manner indicating he was satisfied this would not prove to be the case. 'But, what I've heard tell, the owner being kin of his'n, Ram Turtle's tooken such a fancy to that lil ole bank he keeps a fair slew of his spare cash money in its vault.'

'*Ram Turtle*?' Tuttle gasped and, suddenly, the other three also lost their interest in the scantily attired and shapely woman. Like him, they knew the man named to be the current head of a family which had been very prominent in the criminal activities of Texas even before independence was wrested from Mexico in 1836.[1] Being equally aware of how little protection against reprisals would be offered by Frank Cousins on learning what they had done, if they had gone through with such a dangerous hold up, he swung an accusatory glare at the instigator of the plot and growled indignantly. 'Hot damn, Brock, you wanted us to go—!'

'To go to Boerne and clean out that ole bank,' the "hairy" giant finished, when the speaker refrained in response to a furiously forbidding shake from Cousins' head. 'I'll say one thing. You boys may be long on guts 'n' gall, but you're way shy on brains should such be your intentions. I'd've thought you'd've heard what happened to the last bunch's tried it.'

'What did happen to 'em?' Sims inquired, impressed by the seriousness with which "Grizzly Bear" was delivering the information and concluding the reprisals must have been most drastic to have made such an impression upon him.

'It wasn't *pretty*, nor *painless*,' Front de Boeuf answered

---

1. *Information regarding the status of Rameses 'Ram' Turtle where law breaking in Texas was concerned is recorded in:* SET TEXAS BACK ON HER FEET, BEGUINAGE, BEGUINAGE IS DEAD! *and, by inference,* THE QUEST FOR BOWIE'S BLADE. *Details about an earlier and later head of the family, Coleman and Hogan, are given respectively in,* OLE DEVIL AND THE CAPLOCKS *and some volumes of the* Alvin Dustine 'Cap' Fog *series. Some aspects of the struggle by Texans to obtain freedom from Mexican oppression are described in the* Ole Devil Hardin *series.* J.T.E.

and made what, despite the false beard, the quartet took to be a grimace of distaste. 'They do tell's how Comanches and Apaches sent brave-hearts to see what was left and learn how to work over a man so he really *suffers*.'

'That *bad*, huh?' Dankey breathed, joining Tuttle and Sims in directing scowls of disapproval at Cousins.

'That *bad!*' the "hairy" giant said sombrely. 'Now me, I know a place's'd be a whole heap safer to take down.'

'Where'd that be, "Grizzly"?' Tuttle asked eagerly, and even the dandy joined his companions in showing interest.

'There's good pickings in Tennyson,' Front de Boeuf obliged. 'It's a place about the size of Benson City, but it's a whole slew richer since that gal they call "Madam Bulldog" took over the Hide And Horn Saloon there six months back. What with her running poker games with stakes close to as high as at the Big One in the Silverbell Saloon over to Fort Worth,[2] the bank needs to hold plenty of cash to cover them and it'd be well worth going to rob. Fact being, could I find me *four* gun handy fellers to sit in on the game with me, I'd be right willing to have a stab at taking it down myself.'

2. How Madam Bulldog gained possession of the property and built up its popularity is told in: THE HIDE AND HORN SALOON. *J.T.E.*

CHAPTER SIX

It'll Be Just You And Me

'There's *four* of us,' Albert "Albie" Tuttle said pensively, after a moment to digest what he had just heard. He looked straight at the "hairy" giant to ensure the point he was making did not go unnoticed.

'Yeah, *four*!' seconded Wilfred "Burro" Dankey, showing an equal interest and enthusiasm. 'Which I reckon's how we showed you we was real handy with our guns back to the Davey Crockett Saloon.'

'We for sure *did*!' Barry Sims declared, delivering his support regardless of the glares being sent around by the fourth member of their party.

'Now just hold hard for a minute there!' Brock Cousins put in, as engrossed by what they had been told as any of his companions. However, once again he was becoming annoyed by the way the others were showing signs of being influenced by "Grizzly Bear" without waiting to hear how he felt upon the matter. Normally, unless there were more senior members of the gang present, they would have looked to him for guidance. Regardless of the fact that he shared their eagerness to obtain more money than usually came their way when involved in illicit activities, he had no desire to allow his control over them to slip from his grasp. '*Uncle Frank* said for us to keep out of trouble while we're away from the spread.'

'He did, huh?' Trudeau Front de Boeuf inquired, his tone openly derisive and, so far as could be seen of his "hair"

66

covered countenance, it was expressing something close to contempt over such a response to his hint for assistance. 'Then it looks like I'm going to have to look somewheres else for backing.'

'Aw gee, "Grizzly"!' Tuttle replied, his manner disappointed, darting a glance at the dandy-dressed nephew of the man they were discussing. 'Mr. Cousins's our boss and he—!'

'They do say you can't do too much for a good boss,' the massive young man remarked. 'Anyways, after Benson City, I reckon's how you boys don't need to go hunting any more money.'

'Why not?' Sims inquired, as Front de Boeuf had hoped one of the quartet would.

'I reckon you-all must've got a fair share of the takings,' Front de Boeuf said, although he was aware that the standing of the quartet was low among the other memebers of the gang and felt sure, even in the case of the dandy—relationship with Frank Cousins notwithstanding—their take must have been low.

'We got *shares*, like everybody else,' Dankey asserted, but he failed to disguise the annoyance he always felt when he thought of the way in which the spoils were divided.

'That's how it should be,' the "hairy" giant declared, leaning back on his rickety chair so it creaked alarmingly. 'I allus believe in *share 'n' share alike* when I'm pulling a job and I reckon Mr. Cousins feels the same about it.'

'Like h—!' Dankey began, but refrained as he realized he would be ill-advised to make an open criticism of their boss in the hearing of Cousins.

'Uncle Frank shares it out by what you *do*,' Cousins felt obliged to point out, despite being as disgruntled as his companions over the disproportionate division of the loot. 'He always says that them's takes the biggest risks should get the biggest cut comes time to cut the pot and share it out.'

'So you fellers was fixing to hold up the bank at Boerne to show him's how you're up to taking more risks and getting a bigger cut, huh?' Front de Boeuf guessed, sitting straighter.

67

'Something like that,' Cousins conceded, the suggestion having been his.

'Does *he* know's you was figuring on doing it?' the "hairy" giant inquired, aware the answer would not be in the affirmative.

'Well, no!' the dandy admitted, finding the rest of his companions were looking his way and allowing him to act as their spokesman.

'Brock's Mr. Cousins' favourite nephew, though,' Dankey offered in exculpation. 'So we reckoned it'd be all right with him's long as we gave him a cut of what we took.'

'Yeah,' Sims went on, willing to support the excuse. 'We figured to surprise him!'

'You'd've done *that* for sure, going by what I've been hearing around 'n' about,' Front de Boeuf drawled sardonically. 'What with good ole Smokey Hill Thompson being all riled up over Benson City, him having been concluding to take out their bank his-self, I shouldn't reckon Mr. Cousins'd be a whole heap pleasured over having Ram Turtle meaned up at him as well.'

'Maybe Smokey Hill's got his eye on that bank at Tennyson,' Cousins suggested in a surly tone, without attempting to deny his uncle would not want further problems as he was sure this would prove to be the case. Nor could these be avoided if they were to go ahead with their plans regardless of the new information they had acquired. 'Or the banker there could be another of Ram Turtle's kin.'

'Ain't neither of them so,' the "hairy" giant claimed with complete assurance. 'I know that for a *fact*, 'cause I've checked them out. The only law there's a marshal and one deputy and, on account of some fuss about keeping Garnett's county seat 'stead of moving it to Tennyson like the folks there want, the sheriff won't bust a gut over rushing to help 'em.'

'Sounds like you've done plenty of work on it, "Grizzly",' Tuttle praised, thinking how the same did not apply to the scheme proposed by Cousins.

'It's the only *safe* way,' Front de Boeuf claimed, exuding

confidence. 'Pick where you aim to hit, then check it out real careful. Which's what I've done.'

'Here you are, Mr. Cousins,' Jessica Front de Boeuf announced, having listened to the conversation and decided the time had come for her to help their scheme. She came in from the kitchen to place a cup of coffee and well loaded plate of re-fried beans and *chili con carne* in front of the scowling dandy. 'I hope this's all right for *you*.'

'How about our'n?' Front de Boeuf demanded, as his mother fetched the last of the chairs and placed it alongside Cousins with the air of one who considered she had done all that was necessary.

'You'll find your'n all set out ready in the kitchen,' the "blonde" replied defiantly, producing a spoon from the pocket of her negligee and offering it to the dandy. 'Go fetch it yourselves, or do without.'

Much to the surprise of the outlaws, and to Cousins' relief, the 'hairy' giant did no more than rumble a profanity before rising and slouching across the sitting-room. Concluding they too were not to be included in the preferential treatment accorded their nominal leader, the other three quit the table and followed 'Grizzly Bear'.

'Just you eat all that up, Mr. Cousins,' Jessica instructed, moving her chair closer than was necessary in less innocent circumstances and laying her right hand on the dandy's knee.

'S—Sure!' Cousins replied hurriedly, throwing a worried look towards the kitchen as he felt the "blonde's" fingers moving up the inside of his thigh in a way he would have found enjoyable under different conditions. 'This looks good!'

'I made it myself,' the woman declared, truthfully. Although she had no liking for the task, considering it beneath her dignity, since she had been disowned by her family she had had to acquire skill in culinary matters. Leaning towards him, she pressed against the increasingly alarmed young outlaw so he could feel the warmth of her body beneath its flimsy coverings. 'I cook *good*—but that's not the only thing I'm *good* at.'

'I—Isn't it?' Cousins gasped, thankful that "Grizzly Bear" had closed the door of the kitchen after allowing his companions to enter.

'Given the chance, I'll soon show you what else I'm *good* at,' Jessica hinted. 'Tell "Grizzly" I've gone to bed, will you?'

'S—Sure!' Cousins affirmed, a sensation of relief mingled with disappointment coming as the woman moved away.

'Give it about five minutes, then say you're going out back,' Jessica hissed, coming to her feet and bending her head close to that of the dandy. Pushing up the hat he was still wearing, having retrieved it before quitting the Davey Crockett Saloon, she first delivered a gentle nip and then poked the tip of her tongue into his ear before continuing in an equally low tone charged with seductive promise, 'You never know what you'll find waiting for you when you come out.'

Reaching with her left hand to return the hat to its previous position as she stopped speaking, the woman darted across and entered the bedroom. To the somewhat alarmed young dandy, who would have enjoyed what had happened if he had been less worried over how 'Grizzly Bear' might have reacted on catching them in such a compromising situation, it seemed she had only just left in time.

This was true, but it had come about by design rather than accidentally. While playing upon the susceptibilities of the young dandy, Jessica had also kept an eye upon the door of the kitchen. She had taken her departure when her son, having delayed long enough for her to play her part, had signalled he was ready to return by making a loudly spoken remark.

'Where-at's Nellie?' Front de Boeuf asked, contriving to sound no more than mildly interested and completely lacking in suspicion, as he led the other three outlaws back to the table.

'S—She said she was tired and went to bed,' Cousins replied, hoping he was looking less flustered than he was feeling. He removed his hat to hang it on the back of his chair in the hope of preventing its tilted position from arousing comment.

'She's allus god-damned tired, until after I get into bed with her,' the "hairy" giant snorted. 'Then she livens up and it's me's winds up tired, her being one *demanding* woman. Eat up, fellers, else Mr. Cousins here'll finish afore us.'

'I—I—!' the dandy spluttered nervously.

'Hell, ain't no call for you to get all rattled,' Front de Boeuf grinned disarmingly. 'You should've seen her when we met Smokey Hill Thompson for the first time up to Purdey's. I thought's how I'd get her off my hands for good, but he was way too smart for that.'

'You good friends with Smokey Hill?' Cousins asked warily, knowing "Purdey's" to be a trading post and gathering point for outlaws.

'I ain't *"good friends"* with *nobody*,' Front de Boeuf stated emphatically. 'It just so happened he was there the same time as we was and Nellie allus gets the hots for them's she reckons to be important folks. I'll give her one thing, though, she surely cooks good.'

With that, his manner indicating he considered the subject was closed, the 'hairy' giant sank his spoon into the red, steaming pile of food he had collected and he started to eat. Although disappointed that the 'blonde' was not there for them to feast their eyes upon, Tuttle, Dankey and Sims followed his example. Throwing a glance at the door through which she had disappeared, Cousins wondered whether he should accept the invitation he had received. Judging by what had been said, 'Grizzly Bear' was far from possessive where she was concerned, and it would be something to boast about later, having had pleasure with his woman while he was so near. It was also, the dandy concluded, something in repayment for the less than respectful treatment accorded to him by the 'hairy' giant.

'Happen you're going for more coffee, I'm yelling, "Man at the pot!"' Front de Boeuf announced, as—having reached a decision—Cousins pushed back and rose from his chair.

'I'm needing to go out back,' the dandy replied, knowing

71

what was meant by the expression even though he had never worked as a cowhand.[1] 'But I'll go fetch in the coffeepot af—!'

'Ain't no call at all for you to be making a special trip into the kitchen,' Front de Boeuf claimed, deducing that his mother's invitation was to be accepted. 'I've got me a bottle of that good ole yeller *tequila* stashed away 'n' reckon the boys's sooner have it than more Arbuckles.'[2]

'I'll take *tequila* any day, less'n there was drinking whiskey around,' Tuttle declared and the other two muttered concurrence.

Crossing the room, satisfied his true purpose was unsuspected by the 'hairy' giant, Cousins went out of the building. However, just before he completed the closing of the door behind him, he heard something said which caused him to halt and listen.

'Is he really so highly favoured by his uncle?' "Grizzly Bear" was asking, apparently unaware that the words were travelling further than they were intended.

'Mr. Cousins seems to think high' of him,' Tuttle admitted. 'But you know what they say about him and his clan?'

'Cut one, they all bleed,' Front de Boeuf drawled. 'Which's a good way for a family to be. Mind you, folks could never figure out why Cull Baker so favoured his nephew, Benny and, never being tooken too kind' by puzzles, one time I up 'n' asked him right out the why of it.'

'What'd he say?' Sims inquired, his admiration and respect for the "hairy" giant being increased by the sugges-

---

1. *'Man at the pot!'*: a shout frequently heard at mealtime in a cattle camp. By tradition, any man—regardless of his status—filling his own cup and hearing this said was required by range country etiquette to take the coffeepot and do the same for anybody requesting the service to be performed. J.T.E.

2. *'Arbuckles'*: a brand of coffee so common throughout the range country of the Old West that cowhands in particular rarely saw any other kind and used the name for the beverage regardless of who may have packaged it. J.T.E.

tion of such a close acquaintance with an outlaw as prominant as Cullen M. Baker.[3]

'Well, "Grizzly", he said,' Front de Boeuf fabricated, but with an air implying unchallengeable veracity. 'I favour young Benny more'n the rest of my kin 'cause I know he'll never have the brains nor the guts to try and take over from me.'

A hiss of anger broke from Cousins as he heard the chuckles with which his companions responded to the explanation. His right hand went to the ivory butt of the holstered Colt 1860 Army Model revolver and the left reached just as impulsively for the latch of the door. However, he restrained his intention of dashing back into the building and venting his rage upon its occupants. Even as he was appreciating the dangers to himself if he should make the attempt, he sensed rather than heard somebody close by. Nor was he left for long before discovering who it was.

Having been waiting in the darkness at the end of the cabin, the night being warm enough to remove the need to don any extra clothing, Jessica had moved forward on seeing the dandy emerge. She too could hear the conversation in the sitting-room and, while reasonably certain he would not respond in a hostile fashion, she meant to take his mind off of doing so if she was mistaken.

A hand grasped Cousins by the right bicep and pulled. Turned around, he felt an arm encircling his neck and lips pressed against his mouth to deliver a passionate kiss. Nor was this all that happened. A warm and scantily clad body started writhing against him in a way which left no doubts as to who was subjecting him to the attentions. Leaving his bicep, the hand passed between them to enter the waist band of his trousers. It moved onwards until finding and fondling what it sought.

'Come with me, honey!' Jessica invited in a seductive

---

3. *Some information regarding the later career of Texas' outlaw and gang leader, Cullen M. Baker, is given in:* RIO GUNS. *J.T.E.*

whisper, relaxing her hold and removing the hand when satisfied the dandy was sufficiently distracted.

'Su—!' Cousins breathed eagerly, never having been the recipient of such a sexually stimulating embrace. Then a disturbing thought struck him and he gasped, 'N—Not in the *bedroom*?'

'Of course not,' the woman answered reassuringly. 'Although that hairy bastard wouldn't give a shit should he find us there.'

Taking the dandy by the hand while speaking, her tone having contrived to suggest she was less certain than she pretended with regards to the reaction such a discovery would provoke, Jessica tickled its palm with her forefinger and led him around the end of the building. On being escorted under the lean-to, had he been of a more discerning nature—or less under the influence of her presence—he might have been puzzled by what was awaiting them. By the wall of the cabin, a wide tarpaulin was spread over what he assumed correctly —upon being induced to lie upon it—to be a thick layer of straw.

Lover of her creature comforts though the woman was, more than a desire to pander to such whims lay behind the preparations for the seduction of Cousins. When she had won him over, which she was now confident of being able to do, he had to return to the sitting-room and it was not desirable that he should arrive giving obvious indications of how he had spent his time while absent. As long as they remained on the tarpaulin, there would be no danger of pieces of straw sticking to him and betraying to his companions what he had been doing.

'Are you going to Tennyson with "Grizzly" and me?' Jessica asked, rolling from straddling Cousins' loins after some ten minutes he would remember with erotic satisfaction for the rest of his life.

'I—I—d—do—don't kn—know!' the young man panted breathlessly.

'I'd do it, was I you,' the woman advised, rising and

pulling up the drawers she had all but discarded to give more play to her, now, sweat soaked lower body.

'W—Why?' Cousins gasped, sitting up with an effort.

'Because, dirty, hairy and ugly as he is, he's got a clever plan,' Jessica explained. 'And he's correct when he says how much safer and more profitable it would be than holding up the bank at Boerne.'

'D—Do you r—reckon so?' the dandy asked, too exhausted by what he had been put through to notice the "blonde" had started to speak like a woman of breeding and culture, regardless of the context of her words.

'I *know* so,' Jessica corrected, reaching out a hand to help the young man get to his feet. 'Do you care what happens to Tuttle, Dankey and Sims?'

'Not 'specially,' Cousins admitted, without so much as wondering how she had discovered the names of his companions. Not only did he suspect such an answer was being hoped for, but the memory of the conversation he had overheard on leaving the cabin still rankled. 'Why?'

'Because that's what I wanted to hear you say,' the woman claimed. She and her son had planned to get this reaction from the most important of their dupes. 'And I know "Grizzly". He always wants to fill his great hawg's belly with food and hard liquor when he's pulled a hold-up, and he makes whoever's helped him do the same—!'

'And?' prompted Cousins, hauling up his trousers from around his ankles.

'One good thing about *chili con carne* and re-fried beans,' Jessica obliged, 'Which is what he always wants, liking them so much, they're so hot the way I make them, they stop *whatever else* might be in them being tasted.'

'Whatever else?' the dandy queried, frowning in puzzlement, as he noticed the emphasis placed upon those two words. Then comprehension of a kind broke through and, halting the adjustments he was making to his attire, he went on, 'You mean like *poison?*'

'I mean like *poison!*' the "blonde" confirmed, adopting a similarly dramatic tone. 'I've got some that's strong enough

75

to wipe out a whole herd of buffalo. Within five minutes of "Grizzly" and your three *amigos* having taken the dose I'll put in their food, it'll be just you and me to share everything the hold up's brought in.'

'You and me, huh?' Cousins said pensively.

'We'll cut it straight down the middle,' Jessica promised, and she began to massage her bosom with both hands in a most seductive fashion. 'With more of what we've just had together to boot.'[4]

'By god!' the dandy breathed, staring at the slowly rotating massive breasts with lustful anticipation. 'I'll go along with you!'

'Then you'd best go tell "Grizzly" you're in on the deal,' the woman replied and pointed downwards. 'Only I'd do my fly up first, if I was you!'

4. *'To boot': used in this context, an expression employed by horse-traders in particular to describe an article added free to the price or goods taken in barter at the conclusion of a deal. J.T.E.*

CHAPTER SEVEN

It's Not *Killing* We Want

Trudeau Front de Boeuf frequently augmented the sizeable remittance paid to his mother and himself by wealthy members of their family—on the proviso that they remained west of the Mississippi River—by profits from their various lucrative illicit activities and by gambling, generally with success, for high stakes. He had been convinced by the man hired to teach him about such matters, that the results of gambling were not governed solely by a mysterious and intangible force known as 'luck'. While aware that percentages and 'odds' could be tampered with (in fact he had become extremely adept at a variety of methods designed to bring this about) he appreciated how mathematically calculable probabilities rather than some decision by an obscure 'fate' were responsible for the sequence in which cards left a deck, no matter how well shuffled, or the game was played. Furthermore, the frequency with which any particular number was on top of a dice at the completion of a throw did not vary over an extended period. It might come up several times in succession at intervals, implying some sort of overt guidance. However, as long as the dice had not been treated in some way to ensure this happened, eventually the number of appearances of the other five surfaces in turn would even out this apparent discrepancy.[1]

1. *Examples of how dice can be 'treated' for dishonest purposes, by 'loading' or duplication of the number of spots on opposing surfaces, can be found in the definitive work upon this subject:* SCARNE ON DICE, *by John Scarne with Clayton Rawson. J.T.E.*

When he saw how successful his mother's course of action had proved, the massive young man felt providence was at last showing considerable favour for the enterprise upon which they were engaged. Starting with the required acceptance of a request they had sent by telegraph, nothing had happened to disturb the smooth flow of the scheme which he had outlined on the night of their flight from Benson City and which they had decided to put into effect.

On the night that contact had been established with Brock Cousins and his companions, the precaution of having spread a tarpaulin over the straw in the lean-to of the small adobe cabin had produced the desired result. Although still somewhat flushed by the erotic experience he had undergone, and more than a trifle apprehensive, when he returned to the sitting-room, there was nothing else about the appearance of the young dandy to indicate how he had spent his time. Therefore, his claim to have been stricken by an attack of diarrhea as explanation for his length of absence was accepted without question by Albert 'Albie' Tuttle, Wilfred 'Burro' Dankey, and Barry Sims. Nor, much to his relief, had 'Grizzly Bear' appear to be harbouring the slightest suspicions; although this in fact was not the case and Front de Boeuf had felt sure his mother had achieved what she had set out to do. This summation was verified when Cousins stated his willingness to participate in the proposed hold-up of the Cattlemen's Bank at Tennyson.

One of the most serious threats envisaged by the Front de Boeufs had failed to materialize. Competent and conscientious as the town marshal of San Antonio de Bexar had always proved himself to be, he was not available twenty-four hours a day, seven days a week. Purely by chance, on the night of the meeting in the Davey Crockett Saloon, he had been attending a wedding at a near by ranch. The two deputy marshals on duty had been engaged elsewhere on another matter of law enforcement, and had been delayed in arriving at the saloon to investigate the shooting. The owner, having recognized Cousins from previous visits, had told the other occupants of the bar-room the identity of the young

78

dandy and when the peace officers had come on the scene, the bodies had already been removed and their blood washed away by the swampers. Aware of the important, and dangerous, family which was involved, nobody had denied the story that the gun play had merely been carried out by a bunch of drunken cowhands who had been ordered from the premises.

Unaware of the fortuitous turn of events, the Front de Boeufs had wanted to ensure nothing happened to their dupes. With the quartet won over, they had set about arranging a swift departure from the city. 'Awakened' by her son, Jessica had been ordered to dress and go with Tuttle to collect the horses and belongings of his party. On the way, warning him to keep the matter a secret, as she had done with Cousins, she subjected him to a similar form of inducement in order to further reduce the chance of any of them changing their minds before reaching Tennyson.

Returning with their assignment completed, albeit having taken longer than the other three outlaws expected, Jessica and Tuttle had excused themselves by asserting there had been a need to evade some of the local peace officers. Having put themselves wholeheartedly in the hands of the 'hairy' giant, although Cousins was more influenced by the promises made by 'Nellie', they had not questioned his instructions to leave town separately and not to meet again until well clear of it on the trail to Sequin, seat of neighbouring Guadalupe County. Such was the faith he had inspired that it never occurred to any of them to wonder how a man with such an easily identifiable appearance as that of 'Grizzly Bear' could hope to evade notice if his description should have been supplied to the authorities by the occupants of the saloon.

Nor had there been any objections when the Front de Boeufs, still in the characters of 'Grizzly Bear' and 'Nellie', had joined the quartet just outside Sequin late the following day. The outlaws did not know they had travelled without their disguise in the Rockaway road coach. On being told they would continue to travel in two parties, Cousins and his companions had remained compliant. All had agreed it was advisable to prevent their association from attracting attention and travelling separately would offer the best chance of accomplishing this. They had conceded, just as readily, that it was necessary for the 'blonde' and the 'hairy' giant to go on ahead, so as to be able to carry out a thorough reconnaisance in Tennyson and they had promised to be at the stipulated rendezvous on the day before the hold up at the bank was to take place.

Once away from their four dupes, who they were confident would certainly join them unless something untowards or unanticipated happened, Jessica and her son had resumed their normal appearance. Taking a more direct route than that allocated to the outlaws, they had travelled at a fair pace in the coach. During the journey, the woman had set about making sure she would be able, if the need arose, to play a vitally important part in the fulfilment of their scheme.

Although it was not an accomplishment about which she was inclined to boast, Jessica possessed considerable skill in the use of a rifle as well as a handgun. Fully cognizant with how difficult her task might prove to be, she was determined to ensure she would have the best possible chance of carrying it out. Showing a thoroughness which characterized all her efforts when she considered the end was worthwhile, which she did in this case, she had devoted time and money to attaining the requisite ability.

Having decided there might be a need for such a weapon when they had been debating how their scheme could be put into effect, Jessica had retained the best of the Winchester Model of 1866 rifles taken from the outlaws killed on the trail from Benson City. She had also appreciated that her selection would not make her task a sinecure.

Well designed and manufactured as it undoubtedly had been, the first successor to the Henry rifle had several good qualities. Rugged in construction, comparatively simple to operate, lacking protuberance such as an exposed bolt and downwards extending magazine, with an overall length of about forty-eight inches and—for a barrel length of twenty-six inches and octagonal configuration—weighing nine and a half pounds, it was much more compact than any of its competitors. Offering a full load of seventeen rounds, one in the chamber and the rest from the tubular magazine beneath the barrel, in skilled hands these could be discharged at speeds of up to two shots per second.

However, the Winchester Model of 1866 also had its limitations!

The most serious, from Jessica's point of view, was the lack of power. Required to propel a bullet weighing two hundred grains and with a calibre of .44, the standard powder charge of twenty-eight grains only developed a muzzle velocity of one thousand, one hundred and twenty-five feet per second. This was hardly conducive to accuracy at anything other than comparatively short range. Nor, as the spent cartridges were ejected through a slot on top of the brass frame, could this be improved by fitting one of the telescopic sights which were available.

Realizing how much might depend upon the accurate placement of the only bullet she was likely to be able to fire, the beautiful and knowledgeable woman had sought to supply herself with everything possible to successfully achieve this. Putting the Winchester in the hands of an extremely competent gunsmith at San Antonio de Bexar, explaining she required it for a hunting trip, he had worked upon the mechanism and adjusted the sights to a point well in excess of the state in which it had left the production line. To make the most of the improvements, he had also hand-loaded one hundred rounds with the maximum load of powder consistent with safety and specially moulded bullets. Following the suggestion he had made, while travelling, she had practised with the intention of discovering the characteristics of the rifle before they reached their destination.

Having come to a point where the trail which they were following to Tennyson crossed a wooden bridge over a small stream, Jessica had decided to take one final opportunity of using the Winchester while they awaited an expected rendez-vous with their assistant, Edward Kinsella. Leaving the team and saddle horse to graze hobbled on the Sand County shore, she and her son had gone in search of a suitable target. What

81

they had found exceeded their expectations, offering as it did an opportunity to carry out one experiment which had so far eluded them.

Walking quietly through the fairly open woodland to reach a distance at which the sound of shots would not disturb their horses, the couple had just decided they had gone far enough when a movement ahead attracted their attention. Advancing with an even greater care, they were able to confirm their suppositions as to what kind of creature was in front of them. It was a buck whitetail deer. Standing about thirty-five inches at the shoulder, with a body and head length of close to six feet, it would weigh at least one hundred and fifty pounds and was in the prime of life. With such dimensions, it was close to ideal for their purposes.

There was, however, one problem to be overcome. Grazing on an area of clear ground, there was no way in which the buck could be approached closer than around two hundred yards. This, Jessica conceded, would offer a satisfactory test provided she did nothing to alert it to the presence of herself and her son. Signalling for him to remain where he was, she began to move with great care, anxious to carry out the assignment for which she had spent so much time preparing.

Reaching the position she had picked out, the woman knelt and rested the barrel of the rifle upon a convenient branch of a small tree. Raising the 'sporting leaf' rear sight, which was graduated from one to nine hundred yards—the latter being beyond the range at which even the most skilled marksman could hope to make a hit—she eased the slide to the appropriate setting on the scale. She had been carrying it with a bullet loaded in the chamber and was relieved of the necessity to operate the lever, with the attendant danger of alarming and putting her quarry to flight. With this done, she closed her left eye and the right gave its full attention to focussing upon the 'knife-blade' foresight as it was centred in the V-shaped notch of the slide.

No lover of the outdoors, Jessica was not in the least concerned with the natural history of the animal she was hoping to kill. The thought that it was an exceptionally fine specimen, which would have gladdened the heart of any trophy-seeking sportsman, never entered her head. Nor did she for a moment consider how she was being granted the opportunity to acquire a quantity of tasty venison. All she regarded the magnificent animal as being was a living target upon which she could test her skill with the rifle.

Moving the barrel slightly, the beautiful woman selected her point of aim with considerable care. The buck was standing motionless, quartering away slightly from her position. Despite a general disinterest in natural history and hunting, she knew the ideal position for her shot to strike. With that in mind, she held steadily upon the appropriate portion of the body. Tightening her right forefinger smoothly, when satisfied that all was as she required, she depressed the trigger until it disengaged the sear and set the mechanism into motion. There was a crack and the butt was thrust backwards against her shoulder as the bullet in the chamber was discharged.

Watching through the swirling white smoke which flooded from the muzzle, too engrossed to have noticed the more forcible recoil kick caused by the increased charge of powder in the hand-loaded cartridge, the woman felt sure she had held true. However, despite the soggy 'whomp!' of the bullet striking upon living tissue, she was disappointed by what happened next. A startled and pain-filled bleat burst from the buck. Rising into the air, it took off across the open ground in a serious of bounds which suggested that, if hit, it was not seriously inconvenienced by an injury.

'God damn it!' Jessica hissed furiously, lowering the rifle without even reloading, much less trying for a second shot. 'I missed!'

'No, momma,' Front de Boeuf corrected, after watching for a few seconds, and he pointed.

Following the direction indicated by her son, too angry at what she assumed to have been a failure to have kept her quarry under observation, the woman gave a hiss of satisfaction. Close to two hundred yards away, on alighting from a bound, the buck had crumpled and was going down. Rising from her place of concealment, she started to walk forward and the massive young man followed on her heels. On reaching the fallen animal, they looked for the wound she had inflicted.

'I hit right where I aimed!' Jessica stated, pointing to the hole just to the rear of the point at which the right front leg joined the body. 'That should have found the heart, so why didn't it go down straight away?'

'From what I've heard, they often don't when heart shot,' Front de Boeuf replied. 'We know you held true and hit where you aimed from that distance, Momma, and, if you need to use the rifle in Tennyson, that's what counts. It's not *killing* we want.'

'Hey, Jessica, Trudeau!' a masculine voice with a pronounced New England accent yelled from somewhere between the couple and the place they had left the coach. 'Is that you shooting?'

'Yes, Edward!' the woman replied. 'I'm pleased you've arrived, you can help Tru deal with my trophy.'

* * *

'Tennyson's grown some since the last time we looked it over,' Edward Kinsella announced, taking a folded sheet of paper from the inside pocket of his jacket. 'That's on account of the business Madam Bulldog's brought in since she took over the Hide and Horn Saloon.'

Almost six foot in height, the speaker had the build of a track athlete just passed his prime who was letting himself go to seed. At forty-eight, only frequent applications of a suitable dye retained the black hue of his thinning and longish hair. While still handsome in a swarthy fashion, his face was showing faint lines of age and dissipation. For all that, he still contrived to carry himself with something of the poise and grace of the 'song and dance' man he had once been. He had never reached the upper echelons of the theatrical world and was already dabbling in petty crime to augment his earnings when he had met Jessica Front de

Boeuf. Captivated by her, he had attached himself to her and her son. Serving uncomplainingly in whatever capacity was demanded of him, he asked only to be allowed to share her bed as often as circumstances allowed. Nor, finding him a most accomplished and satisfactory lover, did she raise objections to supplying such a recompense for his services.

Although he was by preference what was termed a 'snappy' dresser, tending to follow the latest trends in Eastern fashions, Kinsella always selected attire suitable to the task he was performing. Sent to carry out a reconnaissance of Tennyson, to discover if any major changes had been made since the last occasion he had done so, he had elected to pose as a travelling salesman awaiting the arrival of samples of his unspecified company's products which had gone missing. He had on a pearl grey derby hat, a not too expensive three-piece dark grey suit, a cheap white shirt from which he had removed the detachable celluloid collar and plain blue necktie, and tan walking boots. Being in Texas, there was nothing out of character about the gunbelt and holstered Smith & Wesson No. 3 American Model of 1869 revolver strapped about his waist.

Having rented a mount from the livery barn in Tennyson, Kinsella had ridden along the trail to the rendezvous as instructed by Jessica. Finding she and her son were not with their coach and horses, he had put to use an unexpected talent for reading simple tracks and had set out on foot after them. Hearing the rifle shot, he had called out and thus found them. However, regardless of the response he had elicited, he had not been required to help Front de Boeuf deal with the slaughtered whitetail buck. Realizing that to take the carcase with them would indicate the possession of a rifle, which it was imperative should not be known, Jessica had changed her mind. Leaving the body where it had fallen, they had returned to the bridge and got down to the business which had brought them together.

'We've been hearing about that,' the woman admitted. 'Has it made any difference to the layout of the Square?'

'No,' Kinsella replied, opening what proved to be a well

drawn map of the town. 'All the building is being done elsewhere.'

'Let me see,' Jessica commanded, rather than requested.

Taking the sheet of paper and running her right forefinger along the main thoroughfare, Vernon Street, the woman stopped at the point roughly in the centre where it widened to form what the citizens referred to as the Square. Having many of the main official and business premises around its four sides, this was the focal point of her attention. Aware of its importance, Kinsella had given each building a number and listed its purpose. As an extra aid to identification, he had marked the combined jailhouse and office of the local law enforcement agencies with a red cross. It was at the right on the northern corner. Designated in a similar fashion, the Cattlemen's Bank and the Hide and Horn Saloon were spaced along the side. Facing the latter, across the close to one hundred yards wide and completely open Square, was the Fortescue Hotel.

'I'd say it's about one hundred and fifty yards from the hotel to the bank, momma,' Front de Boeuf estimated, looking over his mother's shoulder. 'Of course, you may not need to shoot that far. In fact, you probably won't.'

'That depends upon the direction he comes from,' Jessica replied. 'Anyway, we know the Winchester will carry true to further than that.'

'It can with *you* behind it, Jess,' Kinsella declared, thinking of the way in which the buck had been shot by the woman.

'Thank you, Edward,' Jessica replied, folding and holding out the map. 'You've done this so neatly it is a shame to burn it, but you'd better. Is the town busy?'

'Not at present,' Kinsella answered, beaming in delight as he realised he would receive something more to his liking than mere words for his latest efforts. 'It seems all the local spreads have sent off most of their cowhands with trail herds, and there isn't a big poker game at the Hide and Horn Saloon for another two weeks to bring players in.'

'There's no chance of the cowhands coming back before we're ready?' Front de Boeuf inquired.

'None are expected until the end of the month at the earliest,' the "salesman" stated. 'I've been keeping watch and by three o'clock every afternoon the Square looks like a ghost town. From what I've seen, that's when the marshal and his deputy take their rest. At least, I've never seen either of them out and about.'

'Are they at the jailhouse?' Jessica wanted to know.

'Either there or 'tending their horses at the livery barn,' Kinsella supplied. 'I went to the hotel this morning, pretending my boss was thinking of coming for a visit. I made the usual joke about him going to the best place in town while I have to use a cheap rooming house, then asked if he could get in. They're almost empty and there are several rooms unoccupied which overlook the Square.'

'Better and better,' Jessica declared, watching the "salesman" burning the map. 'Now, while Tru is cleaning the Winchester and harnessing our team, why don't you and I take a stroll along the stream, Edward. We can see if there's anything we've forgotten and I'll be able to thank you *properly* for all you've done.'

CHAPTER EIGHT

Howdy, Cousin Jessica

'Dagnab and consarn it,' ejaculated Deputy Town Marshal Herman "Pockets" Hoscroft with seeming irascibility, as he came out to meet his superior on the sidewalk in front of the jailhouse. 'Things're a whole heap too peaceable around here these days!'

'And what's wrong with that?' Town Marshal Tune Collier inquired, swinging around to look about him.

'I'm running scared's how the mayor's just called you in to say it don't need even two of us to run the law hereabouts no more,' the deputy explained, now sounding morose and close to petulant. 'Which being, seeing's how *you* out-rank poor lil ole me, I *know* who'll get to stay on, and I'm way too blasted old to start looking for *honest* work at my time of life.'

'Huh!' grunted the senior municipal peace officer of Tennyson, Sand County, Texas, his manner seemingly disdainful. 'I've never known the time when you wasn't too blasted old for work of *any* kind.'

Just over six foot tall, Collier was a well set up and powerful figure of a man. Nor had forty-five years of life in the Lone Star State, twenty-four of which had been spent as a peace officer in various places, brought more than a tinge of grey to the temples of his brown hair. There was a suggestion of underlying humour about his tanned, clean shaven and ruggedly handsome features. He was wearing a low crowned, wide brimmed, tan J.B. Stetson hat, an unfastened grey jacket over a dark blue shirt with a black string bow tie, matching trousers and low heeled riding boots. The gunbelt around a waist which was more slender than the spread of his shoulders, albeit not quite so much as in his youth, carried a rosewood handled Remington New Army Model of 1863 revolver at the left side in a cross draw holster. Rig and weapon were well maintained, clearly having seen considerable use.

Medium in height, stocky, white haired, walrus moustached and leathery featured, the deputy was equally a product of the Texas range country. In fact, if it had not been for two things, he could have passed for a not too affluent elderly cowhand. A silver badge of office glinted on the left breast of his black and white calfskin vest, indicating his true status. This was also implied by the short barrelled ten gauge shotgun resting with apparent negligence across the crook of his bent left arm and augmenting the walnut handled Colt 1860 Army Model revolver in the open topped holster of his Confederate States' Cavalry style gunbelt. Appearances notwithstanding, regardless of his having long since passed the first flush of youth, he was still competent at his duties. More than one celebrating cowhand had discovered it did not pay to try to hooraw him, but this did not stop the majority of them liking and according him a respect similar to that given to his superior.

At that moment, all in all, Collier was feeling at peace with the world. Even if it had been intended seriously, he knew there was no justification for the concern expressed by his companion.

Due mainly to the presence and personality of the woman known only as 'Madam Bulldog' to everybody with the exception of Lawyer Aloysius P. Scrope (although the marshal was one of the very few residents accorded the privilege of calling her 'Charlie' in private) Tennyson had been growing steadily over the past six months. As was invariably the case when a town could boast of a resident who became a celebrity, as she had done, the presence of the Hide and Horn Saloon's latest owner had had an advantageous effect upon the financial prospects of the population as a whole. Wanting to see her at first hand and discover whether all they heard regarding her various accomplishments—such as skill with a gun, at fist fighting, playing poker, cursing and the ability to drink under the table even the most hardened toper—were true, numerous men had considered it would be worthwhile to visit her establishment. Travelling specifically for this purpose, many had settled upon the town as a rendezvous with business associates. This, in turn, had brought in trade which otherwise would have gone elsewhere and added to the profits accrued by the local residents.

In addition to the interest aroused by Madam personally, there had developed a further lucrative source of revenue for the town as a result of one of her activities. Although less well known outside gambling circles than Poker Alice or Madame Moustache,[1] she was accepted as an associate and skilful opponent by gamblers who played for big money. Shortly after her arrival, poker games with stakes rivalling those of the 'Big One' at the Silverbell Saloon in Fort Worth became a regular occurrence and drew a similarly wealthy clientele. When news of this had got around, men who could not afford to participate for such big stakes still arrived to rub shoulders with the famous players, and they too had spent money with the local businesses as well as at the Hide And Horn Saloon.

An experienced peace officer, whose disenchantment with the soon to be replaced Reconstruction Administration had kept him from accepting any of the more important positions he had been offered, Collier had had mixed feelings over the benefits which had accrued from the presence of Madam Bulldog. At first, there had been trouble between her and Wanda Higgins—wife of the previous owner—who had tried to regain control of the saloon. However, when Madam had emerged victorious from the boxing match they had had and about which the citizens were still talking, this had died away

1. *Further information regarding 'Poker Alice' and 'Madame Moustache' can be found in:* Part Two, 'The Gamblers', THE WILDCATS. *J.T.E.*

without the need for action on his part. It was the increase to the transient population which was causing extra work for his office. In fact, the meeting he had just concluded with the mayor had been to discuss whether at least one more deputy marshal was required to keep the peace in the town. Having decided this might be advisable, it was also conceded there was no need for haste. The selection had been left to the marshal and he had elected to send for a man he knew to have the qualities of honesty and ability rather than appoint somebody who already lived in the vicinity for the sake of convenience.

Bringing his examination of the Square to a halt as his eyes reached the imposing front of the two storey Hide And Horn Saloon, Collier gave a smile. His main source of anxiety over the expansion of the town had not given rise to any of the problems he had envisaged as a result of past experience. Regardless of the often extremely high stakes, the special poker games had not resulted in breaches of the peace. This was, he acknowledged willingly, entirely due to the strict rules and code of conduct imposed by Madam Bulldog. Furthermore, any disturbances on the premises had been handled with competent efficiency by her loyal staff. Only rarely had it been necessary for himself or his deputy to intervene.

Thinking about the precautions taken by the woman to ensure the good behaviour of her customers in general and the players in the high stake poker games in particular, the marshal resumed his instinctive scrutiny of his surroundings. He quickly found something else to attract his attention.

'Nice looking rig and saddle-hoss,' Hoscroft commented, following the direction in which the eyes of his superior had travelled with what was clearly considerable interest. 'And that's one tolerable big jasper driving it.'

'Tolerable,' Collier conceded laconically, or so it would have seemed to a stranger, as he watched the Rockaway road coach entering the Square from the southern end of Vernon Street. Turning his gaze from the massive young man who was driver to the saddlehorse hitched at the rear of the

91

vehicle, he went on, 'I reckon I'll just drift on over and say, "Howdy, you-all".'

'You know him?'

'I know him!'

'I reckon I've seed him afore.'

'Not around Tennyson!' the marshal stated, having been away on vacation on the previous occasion when the young man had paid a visit to his bailiwick.

'Want me to come along and help you say, "Howdy, you-all"?' the elderly deputy inquired, a long association with his superior leading him to suspect—regardless of the apparently unemotional mode of speech—that any previous acquaintance with the new arrival had not been of a pleasant nature.

'Nope,' Collier refused. 'Seeing's it's cooled down some and your so eager to be seen out 'n' about doing your duty, why don't you go 'round to the livery barn and see if there's anybody else new in town?'

'Whatever you say,' Hoscroft assented, assuming an air of long suffering patience. 'And, while I'm down there, happen I might's well go over to the smithy and ask Joshua Gilmore his-self should he want to take on a tired and wored out ole *former* deputy.'

'Do that, happen you're so minded,' the marshal suggested. 'But I'd leave it for at least a couple more days afore I'd start thinking about looking for some other work, was I you.'

'Sounds like I ain't going to be sent off into a hard 'n' cruel world to work honest after all,' the deputy claimed, satisfied the visit to the mayor had gone as his superior had planned. 'And, anyways, I didn't want to have to go work for Josh Gilmore. I don't cotton a whole heap to some of the help he's got.'

'Go on!' Collier drawled, despite sharing the sentiment just uttered by Hoscroft. 'Moe Stern's never done *you* any harm.'

'Neither's pizen ivy,' Hoscroft countered, there having been nothing proveable in a court of law against the man in

92

question over his part in the troubles suffered by Madam Bulldog as a result of which he had had to be allowed to remain in the town. 'But I wouldn't chance rubbing up against none of it on that account.'

'Your trouble is you've got no milk of human kindness,' the marshal stated drily, despite duplicating his deputy's antipathy towards Moses Stern.

'It's kept me alive for a fair spell,' Hoscroft asserted, then nodded across the Square. 'Happen you play your cards right, you could get a tip for helping that big feller tote his bags into Fortescue's.'

'I'll split it with you,' Collier promised.

'Sure, seventy-thirty, like always,' the deputy replied and, satisfied his assistance would not be required to deal with the newcomer, turned to stroll away.

Setting off across the Square, the marshal did not appear to be in any hurry. As he was approaching the coach it was brought to a halt in front of the two storey high Fortescue Hotel, and although no discernible notice was being taken of him, he felt sure he had not been overlooked by the driver. Climbing down, with agility for all his massive bulk, the young man opened the door and held out his right hand to the beautiful and elegantly attired black haired woman inside the vehicle. She too paid no apparent attention to the peace officer's impending arrival. Instead, descending to the sidewalk with all the imperious dignity of a duchess arriving for the opening of the Grand Opera, she stood gazing at the building with something close to disdain. Having assisted the only passenger to disembark, the young man removed the long, light-weight dust jacket he was wearing over the attire of a professional gambler. Tossing it on to the seat of the box, he began to brush off his black cutaway coat and, displaying a similar disinterest in the presence of the marshal, joined her in the scrutiny of the hotel.

'Howdy, Cousin Jessica,' the peace officer greeted, as he knew was required of him. 'I wasn't expecting to run across you and Cyrus in these parts.'

'Why great heavens to Betsy!' the woman ejaculated,

93

turning towards the speaker and showing what appeared to be surprise. 'Will you just take a look at who we have here, *Trudeau*. It's Cousin Tune Collier no less!'

'Yes, momma,' replied the massive young driver, making an effort to conceal the irritation he always felt when a member of the family referred to him by the sobriquet based upon the name of his father and which he thoroughly detested.[2] 'So it is!'

'Well now, Cousin Jessica,' Collier drawled, trying to sound more cordial than he was feeling. 'And what brings you to Tennyson?'

'I trust you aren't asking in your *official* capacity, *Cousin Tune*?' Jessica Front de Boeuf countered, her attitude very much that of a *grande dame* condescending to make conversation with a social inferior whom fate had caused to be distantly related to her.

'I'm not,' Collier asserted, although this was hardly the truth.

'And I hope this hotel is less *dreary* than it looks from the outside?' the woman went on, although the establishment had been painted and redecorated externally since she had last found accommodation there—wearing a blonde wig which she hoped would prevent her from being recognized by any member of the staff. She had noticed as she was approaching, that the Hide And Horn Saloon and the Cattlemen's Bank had also been painted.

'It's the best place in town,' the marshal stated. 'Are you figuring on staying hereabouts for long?'

'We *may* stay a while,' Jessica answered, her manner implying she considered she was doing her kinsman and the population as a whole a favour by admitting even that much. '*Trudeau* tells me he has heard poker for *worthwhile* stakes is

2. *Such was the reticence of both previous generations and the present day members of the Counter family where the disreputable activities of Jessica and Trudeau Front de Boeuf were concerned, we attributed an attempt to cause the death of Mark Counter to 'Cousin Cyrus' as recently as when producing the manuscript for:* Part Two, 'We Hang Horse Thieves High', J.T.'S HUNDREDTH. *J.T.E.*

often played here, presumably in that *saloon* thing across the street. So he wishes to try his luck and you know me, I just dote on the dear boy too much to refuse him his simple pleasures.'

'So I've always heard tell,' Collier admitted, with more veracity than when replying to an earlier question, although some of the "pleasures" to which his massive young kinsman was addicted were rumoured to be neither simple nor innocuous.

'Would there be any objection to him playing?' the woman challenged.

'Objections from who?' asked the peace officer.

'Why from *you*, of course.'

'*Me*?' the marshal said, and continued speaking just a trifle more quickly than he intended. 'Why me? It's none of *my* say-so who-all's let sit in on the games at the Hide And Horn!'

'Perhaps not,' Jessica replied, with a knowing smile. 'But I've heard you are on quite *friendly* terms with the owner.'

'Not just with *her*!' Collier corrected, his manner cold. 'I'm friendly with *all* the law-abiding folks in my bailiwick!'

Although Madam Bulldog and the marshal had come to be on excellent terms, this was an age long before promiscuity had become elevated by a certain very vocal type of mentality to replace genuine effort and achievement as the ultimate symbol of success. Aware that convention frowned upon a relationship which included sexual intercourse outside the bounds of wedlock, they had never allowed their association to pass beyond a warm friendship based upon mutual respect. Knowing that to do otherwise would offer a chance to those opposed to them to level charges of complicity against them, or even immorality, they had taken care to let it be seen their affiliation was no more than platonic. Nevertheless, unfounded rumours hinting at something much closer had been circulated and he was always ready to refute them.

'My dear Cousin Tune!' Jessica said in a placatory fashion, sensing her words had touched a nerve more sharply than was intended and, as doing so would serve her purpose better than antagonizing Collier, wanting to convey an impression of seeking to make amends. 'I assure you that I did not wish to imply there is the *slightest* impropriety in your relationship with the *lady* owner of the saloon. I hope that I haven't inadvertently given offence?'

'There's none taken,' the peace officer claimed, showing signs of being mollified.

'Then you won't object to Trudeau joining the poker game?' the woman inquired, exuding an aura of innocent hope.

Coming so quickly after the unexpected and surprisingly gracious apology, the question placed Collier on the horns of a dilemma. Although not closely related, to one raised as he had been in the Southron's tradition of respecting family ties no matter how loosely they might be, the newly arrived mother and son were qualified to be considered as 'kin'. Such was the reticence of Cornelia Front de Boeuf where more distant relatives were concerned, he had not heard of the wrongs done to her, and knew only that they were not liked by other members of the clan. On the other hand, while he had never received any proof—the incident at Benson City having taken place under an assumed name and gone unrecorded due to the visit by Frank Cousins' gang—he was aware that the massive young man was suspected of using dishonest methods when gambling. Therefore, he was torn between his duty to keep the peace, a wish to avoid trouble in his bailiwick, and a reluctance to show a lack of courtesy to people who classed as his kin.

'Like I said,' the marshal drawled, after a moment's thought, realizing the owner of the saloon was probably even better informed than himself regarding the activities of Trudeau Front de Boeuf and, even if this was not the case, was well able to protect herself against crooked gambling. 'That's up to Madam Bulldog, not me. She'll expect him to put at least two thousand dollars in the Cattlemen's Bank as surety against his good behaviour while he's in town, and he'll have to show *proof* of how much higher losses he's good for in the game.'

96

'We know the house rules,' Jessica stated, nodding as if to indicate approval. 'They are a most sensible precaution.'

'Most folks reckon so,' Collier asserted, without admitting he had reached such a conclusion when informed by Madam Bulldog of the rules she intended to enforce. 'But the next big game's not for two weeks.'

'Good, that will give Trudeau plenty of time to get to know at least some of the players he will be up against,' the woman replied. 'So, provided the hotel proves satisfactory, we'll stay here until it takes place. Do they have any bell-boys to carry in our luggage?'

'Sure they do,' the marshal confirmed, just a trifle indignantly, the question having been asked in a manner which implied a negative answer was expected. Refraining from mentioning the service had only recently come into use and resulted from the flow of well-to-do clients brought to Tennyson by the presence of Madam Bulldog, he went on, 'You'll find a couple in the lobby, Cy—*Trudeau*.'

'I'll go and take a look, momma,' Front de Boeuf offered, confident the disguises employed by his mother and himself during the previous visit would avoid recognition on the part of the employees in the hotel.

'Er—I hope you don't mind, Cousin Tune,' Jessica remarked, in an apparently close to apologetic tone, as her son was disappearing through the front entrance of the building. 'But Trudeau and I feel it would be best if we don't mention *you* are our kin while we're here. It might appear we were trying to capitalize upon our relationship if we should do so.'

'That's all right with me,' Collier assented, having suspected the Front de Boeufs might have hoped to use their family ties with him to gain acceptance by—or, at least, preferential treatment from—the townsfolk. 'I'll likely be seeing you around, though.'

'I should certainly hope so,' the woman declared amiably, despite concluding correctly that the words meant a watch would be kept upon their activities. Not that it mattered under the circumstances, but she also felt sure the marshal would not allow being their kin to influence him on their behalf if

97

they should transgress in any way. Keeping her thoughts to herself, she went on, 'Where can we leave our coach?'

'Down to Pegley's Livery Barn,' the peace officer replied. 'One of the bell-hops will go with C—Trudeau—and help 'tend to it and the saddle-horse.'

'That will be most helpful, although he did say he was meaning to take a ride and exercise it later in the day,' Jessica answered. 'By the by, I wish to put our money into the bank for safe keeping and give references for our financial standing. Will it still be open after we've checked into our rooms?'

'I reckon you should about make it,' Collier claimed. 'Even if it's just closed when you get there, if I know Banker Standish he'll open up should you knock and tell him what you're wanting.'

'My, isn't this a friendly and *helpful* town?' the woman purred.

'We try to keep it that way,' the marshal declared and, once again, there was a hint of a threat under the easy drawl. 'I'd best be on my way, unless there's anything I can do for you.'

'Not a thing,' Jessica refused.

'Have a good stay then,' Collier requested.

'We will, Cousin Tune,' the beautiful woman affirmed, and set off across the side-walk in the direction taken by her son.

Thinking of the conversation as he was returning to the jailhouse, the peace officer wondered if he might be doing the Front de Boeufs an injustice in suspecting their motives for visiting Tennyson. Whether this was the case or not, however, he felt sure the money deposited with the Cattlemen's Bank and which would be forfeit in the event of proven dishonesty, even prior to participation in the big game, would ensure good behaviour from the massive young man and Jessica. Therefore, he was satisfied they were unlikely to do anything to infringe the law, or disturb the peace, in his bailiwick.

CHAPTER NINE

I've Heard About Madam Bulldog

'Hey, Josh, fellers!' Moses Stern said excitedly to the half a dozen men with whom he was pitching horseshoes in the open space between the blacksmith's shop and Pegley's livery barn. 'Will you just take a look at what's coming this way?'

The comment startled Joshua Gilmore and caused him to miss the metal pin at which he was making a throw, the speaker had not been averse to having an opportunity to deliver it. Big, heavily built, with black hair and a sallow, surly and unshaven porcine face, he looked far from prepossessing. The sleeves of his grubby grey shirt had been cut off at shoulder level to display heavily muscled arms and the front was open as far as the waist band of badly stained Levi's pants. As he had removed the leather apron which offered protection while doing as little work as possible around Gilmore's smithy, a hairy chest merging into a bulging paunch showed. Despite the furious glare directed his way by Gilmore, his current employer, he was eager to divert attention from the matter under discussion by his companions and which he found most disturbing.

During the last three months, every time Stern had been in the company of this particular group, the conversation had invariably come around to one topic. With an ever growing rancour, they had demanded to know when—if ever—his half-sister would resume her efforts to regain possession of the Hide and Horn Saloon where he, Moses Stern, had worked as head bouncer. They were prominent in the faction which had taken a dislike, for one reason or another, to Madam Bulldog, and they had all lost heavily in the betting when she had accepted a challenge to fight Wanda Higgins in a boxing bout, and had defeated her. Gilmore, regardless of the fact that he had benefited from the continued failure to evict the new owner, had started to grow as vociferous as the others in the clamour for some form of positive action against her.

The beneficial aspects for Gilmore had arisen when Wanda Higgins, prior to leaving Tennyson on learning that her husband had sold the saloon without her knowledge, had requested that Gilmore employ Stern in his smithy. She had explained that this was merely so that her half-brother could remain in the town while she and her half-brother Leo Wallace, went to Garnett, the county seat, and sought for some means to regain control of the business. The black-smith, regardless of having been on terms of some intimacy with her, would have refused to hire a man he knew to be inept and idle if it hadn't been for the fact that she had agreed the arrangement would only be temporary and that she would supplement the pay he gave to Stern. The proposed retrieval of the property had failed to materialize, but Gilmore had not discharged his unsatisfactory helper. Despite repeated requests from Wanda that her contributions to Stern's wages should be cancelled, he was still receiving a proportion of the money and Stern was just useful enough to be kept on under those circumstances.

Greasily handsome, in a florid fashion, Gilmore was tall and thickset, albeit far softer fleshed than might have been expected from the owner of a smithy. He always dressed as loudly as he had when he had been a whiskey drummer, before he had won his present business in a poker game. That it continued to supply an adequate service was due to the efforts of the former owner who still worked there and whose skill at the trade was equalled by a lack of card sense. He hoped to regain it through the same means by which it had been lost.

100

For personal reasons, although he was no longer willing to try and bring it about himself, the blacksmith was still hoping to see the downfall of Madam Bulldog. Considering himself irresistible to members of the opposite sex, he had boasted shortly after her arrival that she would quickly succumb to his charm. Failing to achieve this when putting it to the test, his attempt to create a more pliant attitude by plying her with liquor had ended disastrously when it was him who passed out and needed to be carried home. Seeking revenge across a poker table, he had once again met his match.

Suffering from a badly bruised ego, Gilmore had once more allied himself with Wanda Higgins. Some time after the boxing bout, he had sponsored the arrival of a tough woman to challenge the saloonkeeper. Although his part in the affair had remained undisclosed, the defeat of his contender had subjected him to a further loss of prestige among his associates and a considerable sum of money. All of which had given him a bitter hatred of Madam Bulldog. Although he had no wish to attempt action against her himself, he was ready to join the others in demanding to know when something would be done by Wanda, Wallace and Stern.

On the point of insisting he be allowed to make another throw, Gilmore noticed how the rest of the group were responding to the distraction. Turning his eyes in the same direction he concluded the comment was justifiable and worth looking at.

The high-stepping buckskin stallion, its rig, and the attire of the approaching rider were all suggestive of affluence, but this was not the reason for aroused interest of the seven men. Although the clothing was masculine, the wearer most definitely was not.

Tanned, slightly freckled, good looking, the face of the newcomer bore a cheerfully reckless grin as if taking delight in flaunting convention by the way she dressed. A low crowned, wide brimmed, black J.B. Stetson hat encircled by a silver band in the style of a Texas cowhand was perched at a jaunty angle on a head of shortish, curly red hair. About five foot seven in height, probably not yet twenty, her figure was rich and full. Tightly rolled, a scarlet silk bandana trailed its long ends over a soft fringed doeskin shirt which was open one button lower than might be considered decorous when one realised the material was already tightly stretched by the mounds of an imposing bosom. From the way her expensive brown striped trousers clung to her curvaceous hips and thighs they looked as if they had been bought a size too small. On her feet were high heeled and fancily stitched brown boots. Around her waist hung a new black gunbelt, with an ivory handled Colt Navy Model of 1851 revolver, butt forward in the low cavalry twist draw holster at the right side. On the left side of her waist belt, which sported a large engraved silver buckle, the handle of a long, coiled bull whip was thrust through a broad leather loop.

'What do you reckon she is?' asked Wilbur Wardle, the short and thickset owner of a store, such a mode of attire being most unusual for a member of the "weaker" sex in that day and age.

'Maybe she's with a medicine show,' offered fat and middle-sized Rudolph Schanz, whose small saloon had lost some of its trade since the arrival of Madam Bulldog.

'It's either that, or a circus,' Gilmore assessed, forgetting his annoyance over the spoiled throw as he watched the rider drawing rein by the water trough outside the closed main entrance to the livery barn. 'What say we go over and ask her?'

'Yeah!' Stern seconded eagerly, always willing to play the "yes" man—even though the term had not yet come into usage—for his employer, but also determined to make the most of the distraction. 'Let's do just that!'

'Howdy there, fellers,' greeted the newcomer and, despite the shape of the Stetson's crown, her accent was not that of a Texan or anyone who came from south of the Mason-Dixon line. However, if the way in which she spoke was any indication, she was completely at ease in her unconventional clothing and accustomed to being subjected to masculine scrutiny on account of it. Dismounting with the smooth grace

102

of a skilful rider, she went on, 'Any of you this Pegley gent 's seems to own the barn here?'

'Nope, he died about four years back, so you ain't real likely even to find him inside,' Gilmore replied, as he and the rest of the group halted in a rough half circle a short distance from the girl. 'But the door's not fastened. Just go in and holler. Likely somebody'll 'tend to your hoss for you.'

'Hey, fancy gal,' Wardle put in, before the advice could be acted upon. 'What kind of outfit're you with?'

'The best kind there is,' the newcomer answered and she had lost her amiable expression. 'It's run by Dobe Killem. Happen you've heard of him?'

'Can't say's I have,' Wardle claimed, although realizing the name was familiar in some connection he was unable to bring to mind. 'What sort of medicine does he peddle?'

Giving a disdainful sniff, but making no attempt to supply the requested information, the shapely red head started to lead her horse towards the double barn doors. If any of the men had been of a discerning nature, their attitude towards her might have shown more respect. Although none of them gave the matter a thought, she was not like the usual girls who travelled with medicine shows. There was no trace of make-up on her face and its tan was indicative of spending much time out of doors. Furthermore, while undoubtedly feminine, her movements had a healthy spring suggestive of a more robust way of life than helping to peddle potions of dubious medicinal value to the gullible. In addition, fancy though they might be, her clothes were also functional and, even though decorative, the gunbelt, Colt and bull whip were just as much the genuine, operative items.

Taking only the basic fact that he was dealing with a girl whose attire implied she might be less than 'good', thus open to disrespectful treatment, Stern saw an opportunity to gain a modicum of approval from his companions. Directing a wink and grin at them as she was passing between him and Gilmore, he stepped forward. Reaching out with his right thumb and forefinger, he delivered a nip to the tightly filled seat of her trousers. Before he or any of the others could respond to what he regarded as being a witty action, he was given cause to regret it.

Releasing the split-end reins, allowing them to dangle and ground-hitch the obviously well trained buckskin stallion, the girl spun around. Rising swiftly and with considerable precision while she was turning, her knotted left fist struck the bulky man on the side of his bristle-covered jaw. Driven backwards a pace by the far from gentle blow, he was unable to halt his retreat. Lifting her right boot, she rammed it against his chest and gave a thrust, causing the leg of her trousers to ripple under the impulse of the firm muscles it covered. Stern, sent staggering, was only just fortunate enough to retain his footing and come to a halt without falling. Hearing the laughter of his companions and knowing it was directed at him instead of in response to his display of what he considered wit, he snarled a profanity and prepared to rush at his assailant.

'Just try it, barrel-belly!' the girl hissed, clearly having deduced Stern's intentions and showing no sign of alarm at the possibility of an attack. As she was speaking, her right hand flashed across, closed around the handle of the whip and slid it free from its carrying loop. Shaking loose the long lash so it was extended ready for use, she continued, 'And I can practical' guarantee to snake your feet from under you afore you've took two steps.'

'See if she can do it, Moe!' Gilmore suggested.

'Yeah,' Schanz agreed, displaying just as great a delight over watching the predicament of the bulky man. 'You go teach her respect, Moe!'

'You can do it!' Wardle supported and, referring to a defeat suffered at the hands of another woman against whom Stern had attempted to launch a physical assault, he continued raucously, 'She ain't Madam Bulldog!'

'Don't let those loud-mouthed knob-heads talk you into starting something you sure as sin's for sale in Cowtown can't finish, *mister*!' the red head warned, her disdain for the entire group even more obvious. ' 'Cause, happen you even *try*, it's *you* 'n' not any of them's'll wind up with a broken ankle, if nothing worse!'

'Well now,' drawled a sardonic voice, before there ~ould be any response to this scathing comment from the group. 'Was I asked, I'd say's how we've got us what eddicated folks'd call a "sitty-wation" here.'

As he heard the remark, Stern was assailed by a sensation of relief. Every instinct he possessed warned that he faced a grave danger. Standing with feet slightly apart and face registering determination, the girl was handling the long lashed bull whip with the deft confidence of one well versed in its use. If this was the case—and he felt disinclined to put the matter to the test—the whip was of far sturdier construction than would be necessary merely as a decorative adjunct to a medicine show, and would be capable of inflicting the damage she had threatened. In fact, should she decide this was insufficient, it could deliver an even more serious injury.

While the bulky man was certain none of his companions would intercede on his behalf, he was equally confident the same did not apply to the new arrival. Deputy Marshal Herman 'Pockets' Hoscroft might not be a friend, but he could be counted upon to do his duty and prevent further trouble. What was more, with the elderly peace officer on the scene, Stern could avoid having to let the others see him back down from a threat he had no desire to face.

'A *situation?*' the burly man growled, lowering his clenched fists and trying to adopt an attitude of genuinely righteous anger. 'That there god-damned *strange* gal hit 'n' kicked me—!'

'And I saw why she done it,' Hoscroft interrupted calmly, continuing his advance until he was alongside the red head. Halting, the sawed-off shotgun resting as usual across the crook of his left arm, he went on with the air of one pronouncing a solemn legal judgement, 'Which anybody's goes 'round goosing she-males, *strange* or otherwise, asks for whatever grief comes his way.'

'I was only funning!' Stern protested, realizing that his reminder that the girl was not a resident of the town did not elicit any sympathy for himself as a tax-paying and upright citizen.

'Seems the lady didn't see it that way,' the peace officer countered, pleased the red head was allowing him to handle things. 'So being the case, seeing's how nobody's got hurt more'n a smidgin, I'd say it'd best be let ride and forgot.'

'Yeah?' Stern rumbled, glancing at his companions in search of their support. He received no sign of it forthcoming, but went on, 'Well, I—!'

'We can allus go down to the jailhouse and see what the marshal reckons, was you so minded,' Hoscroft put in, a note of grim finality underlying his drawl. 'Or you can get back to pitching hoss-shoes and let the lady 'tend to whatever she was aiming to do. Which's it to be?'

'Come on, Moe,' Gilmore ordered, as the bulky man looked directly at him for guidance. 'Let's go back to the game. You can see how things stand here.'

'That's for sure!' Stern agreed, directing a malevolent scowl at the elderly peace officer as he and his companions were turning away. 'And I won't be forgetting it come election time, you see if I will!'

'Sure hope I haven't been stacking up a mess of trouble for you, friend,' the girl remarked and, having coiled the lash while the conversation was taking place, she thrust the handle of the whip through its carrying loop on her waist belt.

'Shucks, no,' the deputy replied, also watching the departing town dwellers. 'I reckon's Moe Stern's forgotten how I don't have to stand no 'lection to keep this ole tin star of mine. You'd think a feller his age'd know better'n do what he did. Now me, I stopped goosing strange gals years back.'

'What made you quit?' the red head inquired, stepping to and retrieving the reins of the buckskin.

'Strange gals,' Hoscroft replied. 'Here, lemme open the doors for you. Happen you're still of a mind to leave your hoss here and stay after meeting such prime examples of our fair city's citizens.'

'It'd take more than a bunch like *them* to make me change my mind once it's made,' the red head declared, and started

106

to lead the stallion into the barn as the elderly peace officer carried out his offer. On entering, seeing he was following her, she went on amiably, 'Now, what I've heard, you're way too *young* and handsome to be *him*, so I conclude you're deputy for Marshal Tune Collier.'

'You called it right's the Injun side of a hoss, ma'am,' the peace officer confirmed. ' "Pockets Hoscroft's" the name.'

'Right pleased to make your acquaintance, Pockets,' the girl asserted, going towards an empty stall as there was nobody else in the building. 'Ran across one of the marshal's kin a few days back—!'

'Which one'd that be, ma'am?'

'Mark Counter.'

'Mark Counter, huh?'

'As ever there was, which some've said is plenty and more than enough. He reckons he could be dropping by when he's done what's taking him real urgent up to Cowtown.'

'And, in case he can't make it, he asked you to come by 'n' say, "Howdy you-all" for him?'

'Well, not *exactly*,' the red head grinned. 'Far's I can call to mind, his *exact* words were, "You stay well clear of Tennyson, Calam. Uncle Tune's likely got more'n enough work on his hands without needing you to add to it." '

'*Calam*?' the deputy prompted, although he could guess at the answer.

'It's short for "Calamity",' the red head explained, starting to remove the bridle from the buckskin. 'And, afore you start acting all innocent 'n' unknowing. Yeah I'm *her*.'

'Who?' Hoscroft inquired, with well simulated ignorance.

'Come on now,' the girl answered. 'A right smart *young* peace officer like you's already concluded I'm the famous Calamity Jane.'

'Well, yes,' Hoscroft drawled, having suspected the identity of the newcomer even though he considered some of the more highly spiced stories about her were somewhat exaggerated.[1] 'I'd just about concluded's you're the famous Calam-

---

1. *Information regarding the career and special qualifications of Calamity Jane can be found in:* APPENDIX TWO. *J.T.E.*

ity Jane. Which being, but without wanting to sound all nosey, mind happen I ask what's brought you down this ways, Calam?'

'I've heard about Madam Bulldog,' the red head replied, then stopped as if she considered nothing more need be said.

'Madam Bulldog?'

'Madam Bulldog!'

'What've you heard about her?'

'Such's how it's reckoned she can out-drink, cuss, fight, shoot and poker play anybody around,' the red head explained. 'Which being, having cleaned up a whole pile of good cash money in the Big One at the Silverbell and got some time on my hands afore Dobe Killem needs me to go handling one of his freight wagons, I concluded I'd sort of drift along this ways and see how true it all is.'

'How do you mean?' Hoscroft asked needlessly.

'Well there's them around's says *I* can out-drink, cuss, fight, shoot and poker play better'n anybody around,' Calamity replied. 'So I just natural' had to come and find out which of us is best.'

CHAPTER TEN

I'm Frank Cousins' Nephew

'Hot damn, Charlie!' Town Marshal Tune Collier barked, for once showing emotion, as he and Madam Bulldog came together at the front door of the Cattlemen's Bank. While returning from a visit to the home of the mayor, he had noticed she was walking with a slight limp and holding herself somewhat stiffly. On coming close enough, what he was able to see through the veil suspended from her Wavelean hat so startled him that, for the first time outside her private accommodation at the Hide And Horn Saloon, he employed the nickname she had made available to a few very close acquaintances. 'Way you were moving, I thought it wasn't but a hangover from last night. But it looks like you've had more than just a mite of trouble.'

Five foot, five inches in height, the woman who had brought so much benefit to Tennyson was in her late thirties. As was always the case when outside her business premises, there was nothing about her attire towards which the most conventional observer could take exception. The garments, a dark blue two-piece travelling costume and plain white silk blouse, were stylish. Without being blatant, they tended to emphasize a build which was less than slender; albeit it of the large bosomed, trim waisted, fully curvaceous hipped, 'hour glass' variety much admired by the male population of the period as the ideal feminine form. While not exactly beautiful in the classic sense, her features were attractive under normal conditions. However, on this occasion—explaining why she had elected to attach the veil to the Wavelean hat impaled by a pin to her piled up blonde hair—her left eye was reduced to a discoloured slit, the right swollen completely closed and the lower of her full lips enlarged even further.

'You should see the other gal,' Madam replied, sounding remarkably cheerful considering the condition of her face. She reached beneath the veil and winced as she gently touched the swollen and bruised left side of her jaw, then went on, 'I tell you, Tune, there were times when I wasn't all the way *sure* I could lick her.'

'Calamity Jane?' the peace officer guessed and glanced across the Square at the front of the Fortescue Hotel.

'Calamity Jane,' the blonde confirmed with a wry grin, looking as best she could in the same direction. 'And, should anybody ask for references, you can tell them from me that there is one real *tough* gal.'

'It looks that way,' Collier conceded, returning his gaze to the buxom woman. 'But, in the name of all that's holy, Charlie, how did it come about?'

'What?'

'You and her fisting it out?'

'She dropped by this morning just after I'd come downstairs, which was a whole heap sooner than I'd have thought she'd be able to make it. She said how she'd enjoyed last night, even though I'd got a mite lucky all 'round, and asked happen I'd like to go for a shooting match between us.'

'On targets?'

'What else?' Madam inquired. 'We didn't either of us reckon you'd let us use Josh Gilmore and his crowd to shoot at.'

'What started you fighting?' Collier wanted to know, remembering the blonde had said after the boxing bout with Wanda Higgins that she would not indulge in physical conflict in the future.

'I said I'd get some targets set up in a couple of days, unless she was in a hurry to be on her way and she told me that would be fine. Then she said she'd come to town figuring to lock horns with me, knock-down and drag-out, but didn't

110

allow it would be fair seeing as how I'm so much *older* than her.'

'Was that *all* she said?'

'It was *enough*!' Madam declared, her manner proudly indignant. 'Even if my gals hadn't been listening, I'd still have taken her up on it. Don't ask me why, Tune. I know what I told you about not fighting again, and I should have had better sense. But just like last night when I took her on at cussing and drinking, there was *something* about that red haired gal wouldn't let me back away from her!'

Having come to know the blonde very well, the peace officer was equally at a loss to explain her lack of self control where Calamity Jane was concerned!

On being informed by Deputy Town Marshal Herman 'Pockets' Hoscroft of the reason the red head had given for visiting Tennyson, Collier had put aside his still not entirely allayed concern over the arrival of Jessica and Trudeau Front de Boeuf while he conducted further inquiries. Interviewing the girl in the room she had taken at the Fortescue Hotel, he was quickly satisfied that she was who she claimed to be. Having heard about her from Mark Counter the last time their paths had crossed,[1] he was equally convinced she had not been hired by Wanda Higgins or Joshua Gilmore—who he suspected of having been responsible for the earlier challenger—to come and force a fight on the blonde. On the other hand, while he had felt certain that Madam would accept other forms of competition suggested by the girl, he had believed she would not allow herself to be provoked into a physical confrontation.

Although Madam had done as the peace officer surmised in the first instance, it now appeared she had failed to justify his faith where the latter was concerned!

Sensing a direct challenge when the girl had introduced herself and announced a desire to play poker for high stakes, Madam had organized and sat in on the game. There were

1. Information regarding the connection between Calamity Jane and Mark Counter is given in: APPENDICES ONE *and* TWO. *J.T.E.*

four other players, including Trudeau Front de Boeuf, but it had soon become obvious there was a personal contest between the buxom blonde and shapely younger red head. Skilful though Calamity had shown herself to be, Madam had eventually proved the better player by taking the majority of what she owned. Then, showing no animosity over her losses, the girl had engaged the older woman in a cursing match. Accepting her defeat by a slender margin cheerfully, Calamity had also failed when trying to out-drink Madam. However, for the first time since coming to Tennyson, the blonde had needed to be carried to bed as well as her opponent.

'So you locked horns, huh?' Collier said unnecessarily. 'But I haven't heard so much's a whisper about it.'

'I didn't want it talked about,' Madam replied. 'She came 'round before any of the fellers had arrived and I had word passed that I didn't want anything said about us fighting outside the saloon.'[2]

'Which it seems you've had your way, like always,' the marshal commented, considering it a tribute to the respect with which the owner of the saloon was held by her employees for them to have refrained from mentioning such a piece of news to anybody. 'Where's Calamity now?'

'Up to her room, at a guess,' Madam replied, wincing a little as she nodded towards the hotel. 'I had Viola and a couple of the gals tote her over and sneak her in after Doc Connel had 'tended to her. Doc allowed she wasn't stove up much worse than me, but if she's up and around already, I haven't seen hide nor hair of her.'

2. As 'old hands' amongst our readers will have noticed, details of how and where Calamity Jane met Mark Counter, her arrival in Tennyson and the name of the saloon owned by Madam Bulldog differ from those given in: Part One, 'Better Than Calamity', THE WILDCATS. The latter was caused by the source from which we prepared the original manuscript leading us to assume it was known as the 'Bull's Head', not the 'Hide And Horn'. However, the various confrontations between Calamity and Madam described in the above narrative were so similar that to have recorded them verbatim in this volume would have been repetitious. J.T.E.

'Did you reckon you would?'

'Sure, if only to tell me we'll have to hold off our shooting match for a spell.'

'It's still on then?'

'I'd be real surprised if it isn't. Fact being, I'm looking forward to it.'

'Damn' if you're not two of a kind!' Collier said with a grin, then indicated the bulging sack carried by the blonde. 'I was wondering why you're so late in coming to put last night's takings in the bank.'

'Some,' Madam admitted. 'Fact being, if I hadn't wanted to ask whether any word's come in about the references given by that big young "Barrington Cholmondeley" feller, I'd've left them in the safe until tomorrow.'

'Go on!' the marshal drawled. 'You didn't know whether Calam was up and around already and wanted to be able to say you'd made it first if she wasn't.'

'I hate a smart-assed john law!' the blonde stated, but without rancour. Having no intention of conceding there was some truth in the statement, she went on, 'We don't often see our fair city's marshal out and about this time of the day.'

'I've just been over to see the mayor and his missus off on their vacation,' the peace officer explained.

'Apple polisher!' Madam scoffed. 'Are you going to put some in, or take it out?'

'Out,' Collier replied. 'I've got a few things need paying and want to get it done.'

Despite having been engaged in an interesting conversation with a woman for whom he had warm feelings and great admiration, the marshal had noticed four riders who were entering the Square. All were strangers, but this was no unusual occurrence since the arrival of Madam Bulldog and the consequent flow of visitors. Therefore, considering them no more than young cowhands who had, in all probability, come to see her, he paid no particular attention to them and opened the door of the Cattlemen's Bank for her to precede him inside.

'I don't see him anywheres around!' Brock Cousins grumbled, glancing about him as he and his companions rode into the Square.

'He told us's how he'd be laid up somewheres close by, ready to cover us,' Albert "Albie" Tuttle pointed out, despite having similar misgivings. 'So you wasn't expecting to see him standing out in the middle of this *plaza*, now was you?'

Darting a scowl at the speaker, Cousins promised himself that he would need to reassert his authority once the hold up they were about to perform was over. Ever since their meeting with the man they still knew only as 'Grizzly Bear', he had found his control over all three of them, and Tuttle in particular, was slipping. Then, remembering the arrangement he had with 'Nellie', he realized there would be no need for him to do anything along those lines. After they had helped him carry off the loot, which would allow him to throw off the shackles imposed by his Uncle Frank, he would soon dispose of their services.

Arriving at the time and place he had stipulated for the meeting, Trudeau Front de Boeuf had not been surprised to find the four young outlaws waiting for their instructions. He had sensed relations between Cousins and Tuttle were somewhat strained, but the fact that both were present indicated neither had spoken of the 'arrangement' his mother had made with each, unbeknown to the other. Nor had his own control diminished during the separation. He had given them their instructions with a clarity which inspired confidence, and there had been no arguments when they were informed of the part he was to play in the proceedings. Accepting unchallenged his declaration that he would be better employed without active participation, they had agreed to all his proposals.

As they were trying to locate 'Grizzly Bear', the quartet had paid no attention to the man and woman who entered the Cattlemen's Bank as they were approaching. However, although there was no sign of the 'hairy' giant, none of them doubted he was watching. With this in mind, each secretly fearing their huge adviser, they concentrated upon doing exactly as he had told them.

Dismounting, the other three handed their reins to Barry Sims. Leaving him leaning against the support post of the hitching rail, saving them the need to fasten up their horses, the trio crossed the sidewalk. As they had been promised, the Square was deserted. After glancing around to make sure nobody was close enough to see and raise the alarm, each adjusted his bandana to serve as a mask. Then, drawing and cocking a revolver apiece, and carrying an empty flour sack for the expected loot in the other hand, Tuttle and Wilfred 'Burro' Dankey followed their hitherto unquestioned leader as he thrust open the door and went into the building.

'Don't nobody make a god-damned move. I'm Frank Cousins' nephew and we're here to rob your bank!'

Hearing the words as she was telling an amused if disbelieving teller how her facial injuries had resulted from walking into a door, Madam Bulldog looked over her shoulder and brought the explanation to an end.

By the side of the blonde, Collier duplicated her action!

As he saw what was behind him, the marshal drew rapid conclusions!

Studying the masked figures, Collier was doing more than memorizing details of their appearances. Recognizing them as three of the riders he had seen entering the Square, he did not consider them any less dangerous on account of their youth. While none looked exceptionally competent, they were handling their weapons with sufficient skill to pose a definite threat. What was more, regardless of their announcement of relationship to Frank Cousins, they looked nervous enough to be likely to start throwing lead at the slightest provocation. In fact, he believed the dandy-dressed one in the centre who had made the claim was only waiting for an excuse to start using the ivory handled Colt 1860 Army Model revolver. If that happened, the other two would join in without hesitation.

With his assumptions formulated, the marshal intended to avoid offering even the slightest reason for the outlaws to begin shooting. He was grateful that only Madam, the teller, and himself were present. While it did not show, he felt sure the blonde was armed. However, she was knowledgeable enough to have matched his summations and would refrain from offering resistance. Returning his gaze to the teller, he decided there was no danger from that source. Despite having lost some of the colour from his normally florid cheeks, the plump and bespectacled young Easterner was standing motionless and with both hands in sight.

'That's playing it the smart way, folks,' the best dressed of the trio announced. 'Uncle Frank Cousins would want it that way. Now you two this side of the counter, turn around with your hands up high. One at a time and *real* slow. You first, missus!'

Detecting the tension which was giving a slightly high pitched timbre to the command, Madam slowly raised her hands to shoulder level and turned. As was always the case when wearing clothing for out of doors, she was carrying her short barrelled Webley Bulldog revolver—which, in part, had produced her sobriquet—in an open fronted, spring retention shoulder holster beneath the left side of the specially tailored jacket. She was confident it had not been detected by any of the outlaws. However, good as she knew herself to be under normal conditions, she had no intention of trying to draw and use it in her present state of health unless compelled by necessity. Nor in the prevailing circumstances, did she expect the marshal to take any offensive action. He was just as aware of the risks involved and would not wish to place her and the teller in jeopardy.

'Well, I'll be *damned*, a tin star no less!' Cousins declared, seeing the badge of office as Collier pivoted slowly and with raised arms. Filled with exuberance over the apparent ease with which the hold up was progressing, and remembering how "Grizzly Bear" had stressed the necessity of establishing his important family connections, he went on excitedly, 'This one's way smarter than that john law son-of-a-bitch in

Benson City, boys. *He* ain't figuring on doing nothing's might rile Uncle Fran—!'

An interruption was caused by a commotion outside!

One of the horses gave a scream of pain and this was followed immediately by Barry Sims yelling, 'Some bastard's shooting at me!'

Startled exclamations burst from the three young outlaws in the bank and they started to look around!

Although he had so far remained passive, Collier knew the time for such behaviour was at an end. Considerable experience in dealing with their kind warned him that, after what they had just heard, the trio were almost certain to be frightened into opening fire. Nor did he have any inclination to wait and find out whether they meant to do so or not. If he was to take such a chance, he would be inviting death—or at least injury—for Madam Bulldog and the teller as well as himself.

'Drop down, Rodney!' the marshal snapped, lunging away from the buxom blonde and sending his right hand to the butt of the Remington New Army Model of 1863 revolver in its cross draw holster on the left side of his gunbelt.

From the corner of his eye, as he began the movement, Collier saw Madam Bulldog was stepping in the opposite direction and reaching for her Webley. Hoping the teller was showing an equal grasp of the situation, he did not dare spare so much as a brief glance to make sure. Nor could he waste time considering the possible repercussions should the dandy-dressed outlaw be speaking the truth about being related to Frank Cousins. Instead, he concentrated upon getting to and bringing out his weapon. There was, he realized, already a very urgent need for him to do so.

Returning his gaze to the intended victims of the hold up, Cousins recognized the danger he and his companions had created by looking away. He also realized it was now impossible to carry out 'Grizzly Bear's' instructions to refrain from gun play inside the bank. As had been the case when threatened by the bounty hunters in San Antonio de Bexar, alarm caused him to react swiftly. Returning the

117

barrel of his Colt to the direction it had been pointing, he squeezed off a shot. Despite the haste in which it was taken, it came close to achieving success. Unfortunately for him, duplicating the result he had attained on the previous occasion, he once more failed to achieve the goal he desired.

Feeling a searing pain as the bullet carved a shallow groove across the left side of his torso, Collier nevertheless completed his draw. Firing at his assailant, he did not wait to see what effect he might have. Instead, he was thumb cocking the Remington and swinging its barrel towards the second of the outlaws who was showing signs of recovering from the surprise they had suffered. Firing at and hitting Tuttle in the head, he realized he had been less successful with his first shot. Untouched by his lead, the spokesman for the trio was already preparing to continue the fight. However, lacking the inducement given to his companions by 'Nellie', Dankey was posing no great threat. Staring in horror, he was allowing his Colt to dangle unheeded by his side.

Moving somewhat more slowly than usual, as a result of her strenuous activities earlier in the day, Madam had drawn her Webley from its shoulder holster. Bringing it to eye-level at arms' length, with both hands on the butt, urgency making her oblivious of protests from muscles which had undergone manipulation by her maid—who was a trained masseuse —she took aim as her assessment concluded the situation demanded. Having decided he was still dangerous, she sent a .450 calibre bullet at Cousins in echo to the shot fired by Collier which killed Tuttle. An instant after her lead had entered the centre of his forehead, the dandy was taken in the left breast by the third load to leave the peace officer's Remington. Spun in a half circle, with Tuttle making a similar pirouette to the left, either of the injuries sustained by Cousins would have been fatal.

Appreciating how desperately wrong the hitherto apparently successful hold up had developed, Dankey had no other thought beyond escaping. His companions inside had both been hit by gun fire from their intended victims, but this was offering a chance of salvation for him. Twirling around as

118

Cousins was knocked in front of him by the bullets, he sprang to and snatched open the door. Dashing out, he saw two of the horses—one bucking and pitching wildly, with blood running from a wound in its near shoulder—were racing along the street. However, Sims had contrived to keep hold of the other two.

'What's hap—?' Sims began.

'Get going, Barry!' Dankey advised urgently, racing across the sidewalk and snatching free one pair of reins. 'Brock and Albie are both down!'

Alarm gave Sims the incentive to obey, and he showed a similar alacrity to that of Dankey inside the bank. Making the kind of hurried mounts they had frequently practised, without ever having really believed they would need to use them seriously, they set the disturbed horses running across the Square. Already the commotion was attracting attention. Men were emerging from the Hide And Horn Saloon, and the other buildings. Some had drawn guns, but none of the shots which were fired did more than cause the fleeing pair to urge their mounts to greater efforts.

Hearing the creaking of leather, after the brief shouted exchange, Collier clutched his bleeding side with his left hand and started across the room. A glance each way informed him that he need not fear further hostilities from either of the outlaws at whom he had fired. Wanting to see what was happening outside, the drumming of departing hooves suggesting the remaining pair had taken flight, he went across to the threshold. Arriving on the sidewalk, he felt something strike his chest with a considerable force. As the impact was throwing him backwards into the bank, everything went black and he sprawled helplessly on the floor.

Having started to follow the marshal, moving as swiftly as her aching body could manage, Madam heard shooting —including one crack of a Winchester rifle—from somewhere outside. Before she reached the door, Collier was precipitated towards her. As he landed supine at her feet, she stared at a hole on the right side of his torso which could only have been made by a bullet. A gasp of concern burst from

119

her. However, she realized that he had been fortunate to a certain extent. Grievous though the blood spurting wound undoubtedly was, it was less likely to prove fatal than if the lead had made its entrance on the left.

CHAPTER ELEVEN

They've Killed *Frank Cousins'* Nephew

Kneeling by the partially open window of her second floor front room at the Fortescue Hotel, clad only in brief black satin drawers and a diaphonous white robe, Jessica Front de Boeuf drew back the smoking Winchester Model of 1866 rifle. As when she had used it to kill the buck whitetail deer, she did not operate the lever to eject the spent cartridge case and feed another bullet into the chamber. Instead, having glanced around the Square to make sure nobody had seen her shoot, she strode swiftly to the bed. Hiding the weapon beneath the mattress, she threw a look at the mirror of the dressing-table. Satisfied that her appearance would substantiate her story of having been taking an afternoon nap, as well as distracting any male questioner, she crossed to the door and listened for a moment. Detecting nothing to suggest her activities had been heard by anybody on the floor, she returned to the window so as to watch what was happening in front of the Cattlemen's Bank.

Taking everything into consideration, despite her misgivings a few minutes earlier, the beautiful and completely unscrupulous woman felt she had no cause for complaint over the way in which the scheme, proposed by her son on the night of their flight from Benson City, had progressed so far. Of course, it had not gone entirely as envisaged. Nor, regardless of there being one aspect neither had anticipated, had it turned out as badly as it might have done in view of the unexpected circumstances.

Keeping watch from the window, with the Winchester ready for use, Jessica had been alarmed at seeing Madam Bulldog and Town Marshal Tune Collier entering the bank shortly before the arrival of the outlaws. However, studying the behaviour of the quartet, she had decided none had been sufficiently observant to have detected the official status of her kinsman. Fortunately, they had kept in mind what her son had told them and there had not been any commotion inside the building until Barry Sims had been given cause to raise the alarm. Much to her satisfaction, after the shooting, the only outlaw to emerge was not Cousins.

On the face of it, the conception of the robbery had offered every chance of success. The observations carried out by Edward Kinsella had established when the Square was least busy, and the local peace officers rarely in evidence. While depositing sufficient money at the bank to make it appear they would be staying until her son had participated in the forthcoming high stakes poker game at the Hide And Horn Saloon, Jessica had learned only a single teller would be on duty at the appointed time.

However, regardless of everything apparently favouring the enterprise, the quartet were not meant to succeed or even survive the hold up. In fact, it was essential to the scheme that Brock Cousins did not. On the other hand, it was equally important that Collier—whose unanticipated presence had threatened to ruin everything—had not been killed in the ensuing fighting.

Having raised the rifle and rested it on the windowsill while the outlaws were dismounting, Jessica had kept watch along its octagonal barrel. As far as she could make out at that distance, no matter what had happened to Cousins, Collier was unscathed as he appeared on the sidewalk. Furthermore, for him to have come out so quickly implied that he was satisfied neither of the remaining outlaws would pose any further threat to the buxom blonde and the teller. Hoping Cousins and his companion had been killed, saving her son and Kinsella from the necessity of doing so, she had concluded her kinsman was rendering the part she was to play much easier than if the plan had gone as was originally envisaged.

Remembering what they had seen on the previous visit to Tennyson, the woman and her son had based their scheme on the principle that the layout of the Square would have remained unchanged. With this in mind, she had visualized the need to have improvements made to the Winchester and its ammunition, then carried out the target practice during the journey from San Antonio de Bexar. As was originally conceived, she would have required these aids to supplement her considerable skill if she was to make the kind of hit called for by their plan.

As things had turned out, there had not even been any need for Jessica to ascertain from which direction Collier would be coming—in all probability moving at a run—to investigate the disturbance. Instead, he had appeared from a known location to offer her an almost stationary target. Having aligned the sights with an even greater care than when shooting at the buck, she had dispatched a bullet intended to inflict a wound which would be serious and incapacitating, but not immediately fatal.

Gazing down as people began to gather in front of the bank, including her son and Kinsella, the woman wished she could hear what was being said. She was aware that the success of the scheme now hinged upon two things. Whether Cousins had been killed and if the faith she had in her ability as a markswoman was justified.

* * *

Similar thoughts to those of his mother had passed through the head of Trudeau Front de Boeuf as he witnessed the arrival of the buxom blonde and the marshal at the front of the Cattlemen's Bank. However, he believed he had impressed upon the quartet the necessity of avoiding gun play if possible so that they would refrain from shooting Collier without cause. In which case, having developed a healthy respect for the acumen of Madam Bulldog during the previous evening's poker game, he felt sure neither she nor his kinsman would do anything to initiate hostilities. Each would be too aware of the danger to the teller as well as themselves. On the other hand, he was just as confident that they would have sufficient presence of mind and gun savvy to save themselves after he had created a distraction.

When the silence had remained unbroken in the building, the massive young man had fired at and wounded one of the horses. Because circumstances demanded the use of his Colt Pocket Pistol of Navy Calibre, he had selected the animal as offering an easier target than Barry Sims. Waiting on tenter-hooks as he heard guns roaring inside the bank, he was pleased to see Wilfred 'Burro' Dankey leaving alone and taking flight with Sims. Edward Kinsella had led the rush from the Hide And Horn Saloon and started shooting at them. Others had followed the example of the 'salesman', ensuring there was sufficient firing to cover the sound of the Winchester rifle used by his mother. Although he had hoped the fleeing outlaws would be brought down, providing they were killed outright, he was not unduly perturbed when this failed to materialize. He felt sure that, having disobeyed orders by trying the hold up, they would be too frightened to go and tell Frank Cousins what had happened.

Having replaced his revolver in the slot of his vest, Front de Boeuf took his time crossing the Square. He had heard Dankey tell Sims the other two were 'down', but that did not mean they had been killed. If either should only be wounded, it would be inadvisable to let himself be seen. Although he had always worn his 'Grizzly Bear' disguise when in their presence, taking into account his massive size, a survivor might draw the correct conclusion and voice suspicions to others. With that in mind, seeing Deputy Town Marshal Herman 'Pockets' Hoscroft approaching from the north side, he allowed the other people making for the bank to precede him. Showing a grasp of the situation, Kinsella had advanced until in the forefront of the crowd.

Although Madam Bulldog still had the veil of her Wave-lean hat drawn down as she came from the bank, it was unlikely that any of the assembled people would have paid much attention to the damaged condition of her face at that moment. Everybody present was interested only in what had taken place inside the building.

'What's happened, Madam?' a man called and others repeated the question in various forms.

'Get Doc Connel here, *pronto*!' the blonde commanded, without offering to satisfy the curiosity of the onlookers. 'Tell him the marshal's been shot and is badly wounded!'

'How about the owlhoots's did it?' Kinsella yelled, knowing the answer would be of interest to Front de Boeuf. 'If any of them's still alive, we'll soon have the bastards dangling on a rope!'

'The two inside are both dead,' Madam replied, watching a man hurrying to where the town's small, lean and grizzle haired medical practitioner was approaching, black bag in hand. Then, turning to the elderly deputy as he forced his way rapidly through the crowd, she was unaware of the satisfaction her declaration had given at least two of her audience as she continued, 'A couple of them lit out, Pockets, but they may have been downed!'

'They weren't!' a town dweller stated, his tone angry. 'Are we going to take out after the bastards, Pockets?'

'You say Tune's been hit, Madam?' Hoscroft inquired, ignoring the question.

'Yes,' the blonde replied, her voice husky. 'It's pretty bad, but he's still alive. Which, knowing him for the ornery cuss he is, that means he's got a fighting chance of pulling through.'

'Yeah, I reckon he has at that!' the deputy growled, deeply concerned over the welfare of a man who was friend as well as superior. Then he forced himself to attend to duty and asked, 'What happened?'

'Four of them tried to hold up the bank,' Madam explained. 'We put down two inside, but the third ran and rode away with the jasper they'd left holding the horses. Tune was hit as he came through the door.'

'One of the two's lit out did it!' Kinsella lied. 'He turned on his saddle and cut loose with a rifle!'

'That's correct, deputy,' Front de Boeuf supported, pushing forward as he knew it was safe to do so with two of the outlaws dead and the other pair already out of town. Like the "salesman", aware that somebody might have heard and remembered the crack of his mother's Winchester, he was gambling upon the other witnesses having been too excited to remember the fleeing pair had not done as was being claimed. 'I could hardly believe my eyes when I saw the marshal was hit. It could only have happened by sheer bad luck on his part.'

'What'd they look like, Madam?' Hoscroft asked, being unaware of the relationship between Collier and the second speaker and, as it was not disputed by anybody in the crowd, accepting what he had been told.

'Cowhands, as far as their clothes went, which doesn't help much,' the blonde replied, moving aside to let the doctor enter the bank. 'I didn't get a look at the one who stayed outside. The other was maybe five-ten, lanky, brownish hair left a mite longer than most cowhands', but that's all I can give you. Maybe we'll get an idea of who he is if we look over those two who're in the bank.'

'It could be,' the deputy agreed. 'Leastwise, I hopes so. I'm taking a posse out after 'em and wouldn't want to have no mistakes.'

'You'll need some of us to ride with you, Pockets,' called the lean and middle-aged co-owner of Pegley's livery barn. 'Me 'n' Brother Maurice'll come.'

'*Gracias*, Davey,' Hoscroft answered and, after another half dozen men had stated their willingness to accompany him, he went on, 'Go get hosses and rifles. Fetch mine along for me from the barn, will you, Maurice. I want to be ready to light out in half an hour.'

'Viola!' Madam said, having noticed several of her employees were present and deciding how she could help speed the departure of the posse. 'Take the girls and put up some food and beer for the fellers to tote along.'

126

'Sure, ma'am!' responded the shapely and good looking brunette who acted as boss girl.

'Now let's have us a look at those two owlhoots!' Hoscroft commanded and glanced around. Without surprise, he found Joshua Gilmore and the other members of that faction were in the crowd, although none had offered to ride in the posse. 'Fetch 'em out here and tote 'em down to the undertaker's when we've seen 'em.'

Led by Joseph Turner, the tall, burly and usually jovial floor manager, four of the saloon's male employees went into the bank. They came out carrying the dead outlaws and were followed by the teller whose face was ashy pale and haggard. While his companions held the pair upright, Turner pulled down the bandanas and exposed their features.

'They're strangers to me,' Madam claimed, having decided to keep any mention of the claim made by the dandy until she and Hoscroft had privacy to discuss it. 'Does anybody know them?'

'Hell, yes!' Kinsella yelled, stepping forward. 'I recognize them from Benson City. They were riding with the Cousins' gang. In fact, the one on the left is Brock Cousins and, what I heard said, he's reckoned to be Frank's favourite nephew!'

'That's what he told us when he came in!' the teller declared, struggling to control a fresh upsurge of the kind of nausea which had driven him into the bank's restroom. 'He said twice that he was Frank Cousins' nephew!'

'Did you hear that, Josh?' Moses Stern hissed, too excited to speak in his usual muted roar. 'They killed *Frank Cousins'* nephew, even though he'd told them who he was.'

'I heard!' Gilmore agreed, listening to the exclamations which were rising all around and watching the consternation displayed by many members of the crowd. Pleased the burly man had spoken so that the comment hadn't been heard by the others, he continued to speak quietly yet with vehemence. 'Hot damn! This is just what we need to get that fat blonde whore and Collier both run out of town. Happen we play it right, Moe-boy, you'll soon be back as head bouncer, with Wanda running the saloon.'

127

'What do you want?' Viola Grant demanded suspiciously, glaring at the person she had been summoned by one of the swampers to meet in the kitchen of the Hide And Horn Saloon about an hour after the thwarted hold up.

'To see Madam Bulldog,' Calamity Jane replied. Wearing an old tartan shirt with the sleeves rolled up above the elbows, badly faded Levi's pants, moccasins, her gunbelt and bullwhip, she moved forward slowly and stiffly. Despite her face bearing injuries similar to those sustained by the owner of the establishment, it showed no hostility as she elaborated, 'I'm not here figuring on locking horns like we did last time, but you can hold my whip 'n' Colt happen it'll make you feel any better.'

'I don't reckon there'll be any need for that,' the brunette decided, after studying the visitor for a moment. 'Come on!'

'Can you get me to her without us going that way?' Calamity requested, as the boss girl turned towards the connecting door with the bar-room.

'Why?' Viola challenged, wondering if she should have accepted the weapons.

'What I've come about's best kept 'tween Madam 'n' me,' the red head explained. 'And it could help happen some folks 'round town don't know I've seen her.'

'We'll play it *your* way,' the brunette decided, but there was an implied threat in the way she spoke. 'Come on, we can go up the back stairs here.'

Accompanying Calamity to the second floor, Viola left her in the passage while going into the sitting-room of the owner's living quarters.

'Hi there, Calam,' Madam greeted, returning with her boss girl. 'What's doing?'

'How's the marshal?' the red head asked.

'He's been hit mighty bad.'

'Too bad to be moved?'

'Doc said he wished he hadn't even needed to have him fetched up here.'

'Then he's not fit to be taken out of town?'

'Hell's fires, gal, *no*. And there's no reason why he should be!'

'What I've heard 'round town, that's not how *some* see it,' Calamity stated, her voice angry. 'There's talk about what Frank Cousins's likely to do when he hears about his nephew getting killed, and it's reckoned he might hold off should he get word you 'n' the marshal aren't around any more.'

'Them *some* being Gilmore and his crowd, I reckon?' Madam guessed.

'That's who started it, right after the posse left,' the red head confirmed. 'How much backing do you reckon's you can count on?'

'All my people,' the blonde declared with conviction and Viola nodded a vehement agreement. 'But this couldn't have happened at a worse time—!'

'God damn it!' Calamity ejaculated, looking at the battered face of the saloon-keeper and speaking with a contrition which would have surprised anybody who did not know her well. 'If I hadn't come here and got us to fighting this morn—!'

'I wasn't thinking of *that*,' Madam corrected, her liking for the spunky red head increasing. 'But Lawyer Scrope, the mayor and a couple more of the local high mucky-mucks who'd back me are out of town, and all the spreads around here have sent off most of their men, all the best hands at that, away with trail herds.'

'We've got one piece of luck, though!' Calamity claimed. 'Mark Counter's up to Forth Worth. You send a telegraph message to him at the Silverbell letting him know what's happened to his Uncle Tune and he'll come running!'

'I'll see to it right away,' the blonde promised. 'How about you?'

'I reckon the best thing is for me to keep folks from knowing where I stand,' the red head replied. 'Should I be asked, I'll allow's, after what you done to me, I aim to stick around and see you get your come-uppance.'

'Thanks, Calam!' Madam said, with genuine gratitude and without a single thought that the offer of support might be other than on the level.

'Aw shucks!' the girl answered, holding forward her right hand. 'I wasn't aiming to leave, anyways. I haven't licked you at gun handling yet.'

* * *

'So I didn't think I'd better send the message,' Edward Kinsella said, having met Jessica Front de Boeuf in the alley alongside the Fortescue Hotel and told her of his visit to the Wells Fargo office. 'But how did Madam Bulldog know Counter's in Fort Worth?'

'He must have sent word he was going to Collier and he told her,' the beautiful woman replied. 'Anyway, it's better he hears the news from her and not a stranger.'

'Do you want me to leave for Purdey's tonight?' Kinsella inquired, the place in question being about a day's hard ride beyond the boundary of Sand County.

'First thing tomorrow will be soon enough,' Jessica authorized. 'Cousins should be there by now as I know he wants to patch up his difficulties with Smokey Hill Thompson and I've sent him word that I've been asked to mediate between them.'

'But will he come *here*?' the "salesman" queried, impressed as he had been on other occasions by the thoroughness with which the woman had laid her plans. Knowing the two outlaw leaders had made her acquaintance, he felt sure Cousins would go to the trading post at her suggestion. 'I mean, so soon after Benson City and with the changes being made in Austin.'

'The changes are why he'll come here,' Jessica asserted with complete confidence. 'If he doesn't, people will start thinking he's running scared and that could encourage witnesses from more than just Benson City to testify against him before a Grand Jury appointed by the new Governor. Oh yes, he'll come all right—And so will Mark Counter. And, by the time the shooting is over, Aunt Cornelia's money will be coming where it belongs, to Trudeau and I!'

CHAPTER TWELVE

Uncle Tune Stays Where He Is

'Come and take a look at this feller, Josh!' Moses Stern requested, gazing out of the open front of the blacksmith's shop and eager, as always, for any opportunity to stop working. 'What I've heard, from the size of him, he might be Mark Counter!'

Three days had passed since the unsuccessful attempt to hold up the Cattlemen's Bank. Having followed their tracks as far as the county line, beyond which Deputy Town Marshal Herman 'Pockets' Hoscroft had no jurisdictional authority—although he would have ignored the point if considering there was a chance of making a speedy contact with them—the posse had failed to catch the two outlaws who had fled. Nor, although telegraph messages had been dispatched to the sheriffs of the neighbouring counties, had they been apprehended elsewhere.

Even before the result of the abortive pursuit was known, Joshua Gilmore and his cronies had begun to create alarm and despondency amongst their already disturbed fellow citizens with regards as to how Frank Cousins would respond on hearing of the death of his 'favourite nephew'. Public sentiment had been divided upon how best to deal with the situation if the outlaw leader should live up to the adage, 'cut one, they all bleed', as he had in the past, and the faction opposed to Madam Bulldog had done all they could to fan higher the flames of dissent. Claiming the escaping bank

132

raiders would be speeding to Cousins with the news, they had spread stories of what had happened to other towns unfortunate enough to have aroused the animosity of the evil and bloodthirsty clan he led. In this, they had been helped by Edward Kinsella who had—on the night before he left, unbeknown to them, to make sure Cousins was informed of the incident—described in gory detail, while in their company at Rudolph Schanz's small saloon, what he was supposed to have seen at Benson City.

With the passing of time, although there had been only vague and unconfirmed rumours that Cousins was aware of his nephew's death and intended to come and avenge it, the efforts of the faction had begun to produce results. A few of the population were solidly aligned behind Madam Bulldog and Town Marshal Tune Collier. Others, including some generally inclined to be well disposed towards the buxom blonde, had taken a different point of view. Not only did they think of the possible consequences to themselves and their property should the outlaws arrive, but they had been reminded by Gilmore's cronies of how their hopes of having the status of county seat transferred from Garnett to Tennyson would almost certainly be affected adversely by such an incident. Therefore, they had been willing to listen to suggestions for how the problem might be solved.

Faced by growing hints and even a few open demands to have his superior sent to Garnett, or elsewhere, for 'safety' and to order Madam to 'take a long vacation' on the same pretext, Hoscroft had refused to do either. Despite knowing who was responsible for the uncertainty and alarm, he had been unable to prove it and was aware that any attempt to confront them would do more harm than good unless backed by solid evidence. However, he had been able to appreciate the feelings of the waverers and felt sure most of them would rally around if they had a stronger leadership than he was capable of providing.

Much to the satisfaction of Gilmore's faction, this had not been forthcoming. Collier was still under sedation and too ill to take command. Attempts to recall the mayor, Lawyer

133

Aloysius P. Scrope and the other influential friends of the blonde, whose presence would have had at least a stiffening effect, had been unsuccessful. While the local ranchers had offered backing, they were unable to provide many men and none had the requisite qualities of leadership.

Nor, even more to the satisfaction of the blacksmith and his cronies, had there been any reply from Mark Counter in answer to the telegraph message sent by Madam Bulldog. They were aware that his arrival might ruin all their hopes for regaining control of the Hide And Horn Saloon and seeing its owner and Collier, for whom they had no liking on account of his firm and incorruptible handling of the law in the town, removed. Even if he arrived unaccompanied by the other members of the OD Connected ranch's already legendary floating outfit, his reputation and presence might have helped pull sufficient of the population together to have put their ambitions in jeopardy.

'I shouldn't reckon that's him!' the blacksmith decided, sounding relieved, having hurried over to stand by his lazy employee and studied the newcomer for a few seconds. 'A feller that hefty couldn't've got here this quick from Fort Worth. Anyways, Counter wouldn't've come alone. He'd have at least Dusty Fog and the Ysabel Kid along to back his play, they're *always* together. Top of which, that jasper's dressed a whole heap too fine and costly for a working cownurse even if he is likely pulling down a top hand's pay.'

'Who do you reckon he is, then?' Stern inquired, deciding there was some justification for all the conclusions drawn by the blacksmith.

'Could be some rich rancher's son who hasn't heard about Frank Cousins' nephew getting made wolf bait and come like so many more of 'em to ogle that fat blonde tail peddler at the Hide And Horn,' Gilmore guessed. 'Or, going by that fancy fast draw rig and Army Colts, he might be one of Cousins' men sent to scout the lie of the land afore the rest of 'em get here.'

'We could go over and ask,' Stern suggested, watching the man they were discussing making for Pegler's livery barn.

'Like hell we will!' the blacksmith refused. 'If he is from Cousins, he'd not take kind' to questions like that. So get back to work. We'll soon enough find what he's come for.'

'What if he is Counter?' Stern inquired, being reluctant to do as he was told.

'If he is,' Gilmore replied, looking pointedly at the task he had assigned to his idle employee. 'Alvin Cordby's going to earn some of that money Dolph Schanz's got from me to hire him.'

* * *

Oblivious of the interest his arrival was creating, Mark Counter came to a halt outside Pegler's livery barn. Although all of the three horses upon which he had ridden relay from Fort Worth to Tennyson were large and up to carrying his far from inconsiderable weight, they were showing signs of having been hard pushed. However, despite one deduction made by Gilmore, his skill at equestrian matters had allowed him to make the journey swiftly enough for him to have reached his destination in such a short time. Being a light rider, his great size notwithstanding, he was able to sit whichever animal he had been currently using in a way which took far less out of it physically than would a smaller person who lacked his competence.

Nor had the blacksmith been any more correct when assuming Mark would be accompanied by the two men with whom his name was most frequently associated and in whose company he was generally found. While there was much work needing to be done at the OD Connected ranch, its owner, General Jackson Baines 'Ole Devil' Hardin, C.S.A., would have allowed Captain Dustine Edward Marsden 'Dusty' Fog and the Ysabel Kid to ride with him if it had been necessary when he received the telegraph message asking him to meet an attorney who handled much legal business for members of his family in Fort Worth, on a matter of great urgency. Believing the meeting would not require their presence, Mark had declined the offer of their

135

company. Still unaware that he had been tricked into making the journey by Jessica and Trudeau Front de Boeuf, when he had heard that his Uncle Tune needed his assistance, he had set out for Tennyson without waiting for the lawyer to reach Fort Worth from San Antonio de Bexar. As there had been no information regarding the need for his presence, it was his intention to study the situation and then decide whether to telegraph for his *amigos* to come and join him.

In one respect, Gilmore had guessed correctly. Mark's father was a very wealthy rancher. On the other hand, despite the way in which he was dressed, he was a working cowhand.

Even showing some signs of having travelled far and fast, a point overlooked by the blacksmith and Stern, Mark presented a picture Frederic Remington or many another artist would have taken pleasure in putting on canvas. Three inches over six foot in height, with neatly barbered curly golden blond hair and a clean shaven, tanned, almost classically handsome face, he had once been described as looking like an Ancient Greek god who had elected to wear the attire of a Texas' cowhand instead of a flowing white robe and sandals. His shoulders had a tremendous spread, with the torso slimming down to a slender waist and long, powerful straight legs. Yet, even tired as he clearly was, he gave no suggestion of being slow, clumsy, or awkward. Rather the opposite, in fact, although neither of the men watching his arrival were sufficiently discerning to take this point into account.

The misconception about the attire worn by the blond giant was easily explained. Although employed as a cowhand on the OD Connected ranch, he was sufficiently wealthy in his own right to indulge his sartorial tastes. His white Stetson had a leather band with silver conchas around its crown. Tightly rolled, the scarlet bandana trailing long ends over his massive chest was silk. His tan coloured shirt and yellowish-brown Nankeen trousers, the cuffs of the legs hanging outside top quality high heeled and sharp toed tan boots with elaborate stitching, were of the best materials and clearly

136

tailored for him. Such an excellent fit could never have come ready-made from the shelves of a store. Furthermore, a habit of neatness had led to his washing, shaving and changing into garments which did not show the effects of the journey shortly before reaching his destination.

Swinging from the costly, yet functional, low horned, double girthed saddle of the bloodbay stallion, Mark hitched his excellently made brown *buscadero* gunbelt so the matched ivory handled Colt 1860 Army Model revolvers in its fast draw holsters settled comfortably. Eager as he was to go in search of his uncle, his upbringing was such that he would not leave his horses untended to do so. Leading them into the livery barn, he found it had only one human occupant and guessed this was the hostler.

'Howdy, *amigo*,' the blond giant greeted, his deep voice having the accent of a well educated Texan. Glancing around, he noticed the buckskin stallion was present which he had seen Calamity Jane riding and continued, 'I'll take three of those empty stalls, happen they're going.'

'Use any three you've a mind, friend,' replied David Humphrey. 'Those hosses of your'n look like they've done some travelling.'

'They always do after they've been toting my lard around for a spell,' Mark asserted, deciding against mentioning the animals had brought him from Fort Worth in only three days. 'I'd be obliged happen you'd help me with one of them.'

'I can likely do better'n that,' Humphrey claimed. 'You want me too, I'll call Brother Maurice offen the backhouse to help me 'tend to all three.'

'No offence, mind,' the blond giant drawled, indicating the horse which was his own property whereas the others had been hired in Fort Worth. 'But I'll see to the bloodbay myself.'

'Was hoping you'd say that, he don't look like he'd cotton to being handled by a stranger,' the hostler stated with a grin, and went to the side door to call for his brother. While he was doing so, his customer led the bloodbay into a stall near the

137

buckskin and, returning, he pointed to the brand it carried. 'I read that's R Over C. Can't bring the outfit to mind, though.'

'It's only a little-bitty spread down to the Big Bend country,' Mark drawled and looked around the barn. 'You don't seem to be over busy.'

'Never are at this time of the year,' Humphrey answered, being too range-wise to make any attempt to satisfy his curiosity in a more direct fashion.

While the blond giant had given the general location of the ranch owned by his father, Big Ranse Counter, this was not over informative, as the Big Bend country was an enormous region with many spreads within its bounds. Furthermore, by no stretch of imagination could the R Over C qualify for the description 'little-bitty'. It was, in fact, accounted large even for the Lone Star State.

There was a sound reason, Mark considered, to be reticent. The message which had brought him to Tennyson had said only that Uncle Tune was seriously wounded, needed help badly and for him to come as quickly as possible. Knowing Collier was generally popular in the town, he was equally aware that not every member of the community subscribed to the sentiment. Therefore, until he had learned more about the situation and the feelings of the man with whom he was talking, he was disinclined to supply information about himself.

Being on good terms with the injured marshal, Humphrey was just as wary. Although he knew more than his question implied about the R Over C ranch, and was aware of the relationship between its owner and Collier, he did not overlook the possibility of this leading him into indiscretion. Unknowingly, he was forming similar conclusions to those of Gilmore and, having been able to make a closer examination of the subject, had added to them. As two of the horses bore the brand of the best livery stable in Fort Worth, which charged rental prices beyond the reach of any but the wealthy, it seemed likely the blond giant had come from that city. However, this could not be regarded as undisputable proof of identity. He might have been sent by Cousins and supplied with a horse stolen from the *remuda* of the R Over C ranch at some time in the past to create the impression that he was Mark Counter.

With such a possibility in mind, the hostler was on his guard. While he, his younger brother and the newcomer were taking care of the horses, he sought to solve the mystery in a way within the bounds of range country etiquette. However, by the time the task was completed, he found himself no better informed. The blond giant had expressed interest on being informed of the confrontations between Madam Bulldog and Calamity Jane, admitting to having heard of both, he had given no indication of knowing either. Nor was anything said to imply he was aware of the thwarted bank hold up, which was correct as the news had not reached Fort Worth before he left. Humphrey was not able to raise the matter. With the work on the animals completed, the big blond asked for and was given permission to use the backhouse.

'Who do you reckon he is, Davey?' Maurice Humphrey inquired, having deduced what his brother was trying to do.

'I dunno, damn it!' the older man replied. 'Happen he is Mark Counter, where's Cap'n Fog 'n' the Ysabel Kid?'

'Was just thinking that,' the younger brother admitted. 'So he could be one of Cousins' men.'

'He could be,' David Humphrey said quietly and pensively. 'One thing's for sure. Fancy dresser or not, I'd sooner have him with me than again' me!'

* * *

'Have you come for a rig to get him out of town, Doc?' Joshua Gilmore demanded, having emerged from the blacksmith's shop with Moses Stern following on his heels at the sight of the local medical practitioner making for the livery barn.

'I *haven't*!' Doctor Henry Connel stated bluntly, his small size and belligerent demeanour making him seem like a fighting cock faced by a couple of grizzly bears. 'Are *you* telling me that's what I should do?'

'I'm not *telling* you to do *nothing*!' Gilmore countered, always wary where committing himself to anything controversial was concerned. 'It ain't's I don't respect Tune Collier, but Frank Cousins's sent word that he's coming after them responsible for his nephew being killed and you know what *that* means!'

'I know what you and your bunch are!' Connel asserted, his tone contemptuous, although he was silently cursing whoever had been responsible for the story to which the blacksmith was referring making the rounds. 'Should you have heard Frank Cousins said for Tune to be strung offen a cottonwood limb, you'd be wanting to do it!'

Listening to the conversation as he was emerging from the backhouse, Mark Counter did not pause to strap on the gunbelt he had removed. Instead, draping it across his left shoulder, he walked forward quickly.

'Now you know we wouldn't go saying any such thing!' Gilmore objected, but without any great conviction. Too engrossed in trying to present the best possible motives to notice the blond giant was approaching, he went on, 'All we want for you to do is put Tune in your rig and, seeing's how the sheriff's sent word he can't spare any men to get up here and protect him, take him down to Garnett where it'll be done for him.'

'And, like I said when it was first suggested,' the doctor replied. 'Tune wouldn't last a mile, condition he's in, much less all the way to Garnett. Which being, he's staying where he is.'

'Excuse me, gentlemen,' Mark put in, his voice mild and polite, before either of the bulky men could take the matter any further. 'Are you-all discussing Marshal Tune Collier of this town?'

'Who's asking?' Moses Stern demanded, swinging his gaze to the speaker.

'My name, *sir*, is Trudeau Front de Boeuf,' the blond giant introduced, unaware that his cousin was in the vicinity. Hiding a faint amusement over wondering what the more strait-laced members of the family would think about his

140

adopting the name of his less than respectable kinsman, he continued in a similar tone. 'And I really must *insist* that, in view of what the good doctor here has said, Uncle Tune stays where he is!'

'*You* insist, do you?' Stern snarled menacingly, the name supplied the blond giant meaning nothing to him as it was not being used in Tennyson by its owner.

'I most certainly *do*!' Mark agreed and continued to walk in the direction of the doctor, which meant he had to pass the man who had addressed him.

To Connel, knowing the pair with whom they were dealing, it seemed the blond giant was committing a serious error in tactics!

CHAPTER THIRTEEN

The Badge Should Help You

'Then, by god!' Moses Stern snarled, confirming the supposition of Doctor Henry Connel as he reached for and grasped the right arm of the newcomer. 'You'd best quick change your son-of-a-bitching mind!'

Wanting to make a good impression upon his nominal employer, whose antipathy towards him had increased due to his half-sister having declined to take an active participation in the latest attempt to dispose of Madam Bulldog, the burly hard-case had thought there was an easy way to do so. Despite having been in the saddle for the greater part of three days, having performed his ablutions and changed into clean clothing before reaching Tennyson that afternoon, the blond giant was presenting a dandified appearance. Certainly there was nothing about him to suggest he had made the journey from Fort Worth in such a short time. Taken with the cultured timbre he had given his voice, this had caused Stern—who was never over-discerning—to consider him as nothing more than a wealthy and pampered young Southron trying to gain acclaim by coming to the rescue of a kinsman in distress and who would be easy meat.

'Please take your *grubby* hand off my sleeve!' Mark Counter requested and, as he still considered it advisable to avoid his true identity being discovered by the blacksmith —who he knew had never been on good terms with his uncle —he contrived to sound more querulous than demanding. 'You are *crushing* the material!'

'I'll *crush* your god-damned head!' Stern threatened.

Even as the burly hard-case was releasing the arm, he realized what had been puzzling him. Regardless of how his intended victim might look and speak, the bicep he had grasped was of a size and hardness exceeding his own. However, trying to ignore the misgivings aroused by the discovery, he drew back his right fist and threw a punch. While in residence at Tennyson, he had acquired something of a reputation as a fighting man and many of the male population would have felt at a disadvantage against him on this account.

Unfortunately for Stern, Mark did not live in Tennyson!

Therefore, the blond giant had not heard of his would be assailant's reputation. Nor would he have been in the least impressed if he had. Rising fast, while he was allowing the gunbelt to slip under control from over his left shoulder, his right hand deflected the oncoming punch and the other shot out. Much to Stern's astonishment, he not only failed to reach his objective but he caught a blow which propelled him backwards and from his feet.

Staring at his unsatisfactory employee as he reeled past and went down, Joshua Gilmore let out a snarl and charged into the attack. Loyalty to Stern was not his motive. He was prompted by a desire to prevent the newcomer from gaining credit which might help increase support for Town Marshal Tune Collier.

Although the blacksmith made no attempt to keep in the peak of physical condition, he had at one time fought with moderate success in the bare-knuckle prize ring and he advanced in the fist-flying style which had served him so well. He hit nothing except empty air. Having learned the 'noble art' in a different, more scientific and effective school, Mark weaved aside at the last moment. Clipping the unguarded jaw smoothly with his right hand, the left followed to complete the damage already inflicted. Caught twice at the same side of the head, with a force which caused him to have the impression that bright lights were erupting from it,

143

Gilmore was knocked sideways in a sprawl which ended with him alighting on hands and knees.

Given the opportunity, Stern had wasted no time in lurching upright. Continuing to call upon all the speed he could muster, he rushed over to throw his arms around the comparatively slender waist of the blond giant and clamped on one of his favourite holds. A grunt of pain burst from Mark, for Stern had developed the crushing 'bear hug' to a fine art. Watching, Connel was alarmed for the safety of the man who had claimed to be related to Tune Collier. On other occasions when the burly hard-case had gained such a grip, the recipients had wound up by being brought to the surgery with badly crushed ribs and whatever subsequent injuries he had inflicted upon them.

Feeling the enormous constriction of the powerful encircling arms, Mark was aware of the danger. Instinctively, he rammed his hands under the bristle covered jaw of his assailant. Such was the enormous strength he was capable of exerting, he prevented the other from being able to continue the pressure. However, he was unable to break the bear hug hold. It became a trial of strength pure and simple. The blond giant was convinced he could out-do his attacker, but the second man was starting to get up and he knew he would be unable to cope with both of them while encumbered in such a fashion.

Remembering how he had seen Dusty Fog escape from a similar grip, Mark removed his hands from the already forced back head of the hard-case. Raising them as the crushing was being recommenced, he chopped downwards so their edges bit against either side of Stern's thick neck. A strangled squawk of pain burst from the hard-case and, loosing the hold, he started to blunder half choking away from the blond giant. Following him, Mark subjected him to a punch just below the *solar plexus* which far exceeded any such attack he had ever suffered. Doubling over, hands reaching instinctively for the stricken area, his knees began to buckle. He was not allowed to go all the way down. Upwards lashed the blond giant's other fist. Catching Stern beneath the chin, it

144

lifted him erect and pitched him, unconscious and helpless, on to his back.

Hoping to be able to launch an attack before the newcomer was able to counter it, Gilmore lunged forward like a sprinter starting a foot-race. Much to his dismay, he saw the big Southron was swinging towards him before he was within reaching distance with his outstretched hands. He felt his right wrist being gripped with a force like the closing jaws of a bear-trap. Pivoting underneath while raising the trapped arm, his intended victim gave a powerful twisting downwards wrench upon it. A wail of consternation burst from him as his feet left the ground. Turning an involuntary half circle through the air, he came down supine with a crash which drove all the air from his lungs.

Although breathless, the blacksmith was still conscious. Knowing how he would treat an opponent in a similar position, he gazed up in horror at the man he had thought would prove an easy victim and he tried to plead for the attack he believed would be delivered to be held off. It was not launched. Looking down at his frightened face for a few seconds, although it seemed like hours to him, the blond giant gave a nod of satisfaction and turned away.

'You said Uncle Tune's hurt real bad, sir?' Mark inquired, retrieving and buckling on the gunbelt.

'Real bad's the word for it,' Connel confirmed. 'I wish I didn't have to leave him, but there's a young woman at the Leaning J who's about due to foal down with her first and I've a suspicion's it's not going to come easy.'

'He'd understand,' the blond giant claimed, accompanying the doctor towards the livery barn. 'Where-all's he at?'

'The Hide And Horn Saloon,' Connel replied without hesitation, noticing a change had come to the other's voice and the apparently querulous air had gone. 'Madam Bulldog had him taken there and he's in one of her private rooms. Do you know what's coming off around here?'

'All the message I got in Cowtown said was Uncle Tune'd been shot bad and needed help,' Mark admitted. 'But, going by what those butt-dragging yahoos said just now, I've a notion it goes *some* beyond that.'

'It goes *way* beyond just that!' the doctor corrected, then realized the telegraph message sent by Madam Bulldog had not been addressed to the name given by the blond giant. 'Are you on your lonesome, Mr. *Front de Boeuf?*'

'I didn't think it would be safe to bring Au—my *mother* with me,' Mark answered, having decided against revealing his identity with one attacker still able to hear what was being said, even though his uncle had always spoken of the doctor as a good friend.

'Did you reckon the same about your Uncle Dusty and your Uncle Kid?' Connel asked with a grin, taking no offence over what he considered to be a sensible precaution if his assumptions with regards to the identity of the blond giant should be correct.

'Yep, them being so delicate and gently reared,' Mark replied. 'But I'm getting another of my sneaky lil ole notions tells me I should've asked them to meet me here!'

* * *

'Just you stay right there, Tune Collier!' Madam Bulldog ordered, escorting the man she had summoned from Fort Worth into the smaller of the bedrooms in her private accommodation on the second floor of the Hide And Horn Saloon. 'I know you're all woke up bright eyed and bushy tailed at last, but you're a long ways short from ready to be wanting to go drinking and carousing because you've got kin calling.'

'M—Mark!' the peace officer gasped, the reference to his condition being a considerable exaggeration. He refrained from attempting to lift himself into at least a sitting position, the effort having proved too much for him. 'H—How the devil did y—?'

'On three real tired horses,' the blond giant replied. Although the drapes at the windows were drawn, there was sufficient light for him to see his uncle was far from having

146

thrown off the effects of what Doctor Connel had said was a close to fatal wound. 'They didn't start out that way, but they seemed to wind up like it.'

'Horses *always* wind up tired after they've toted any of you lard-fat Counters around for a spell,' Collier claimed in a weak voice, but showing something of his usual spirits and managing to lift his right hand just high enough to be shaken. 'I can't say I'm sorry to see you, for once, Mark-boy. Are Cap'n Fog and the Kid along?'

'I wish they were,' the blond giant admitted wryly. 'Dusty in particular!'

'They couldn't get here before Cousins, I reckon?' Madam estimated, then turned her still bruised face as she realized how the words could be construed and went on in contrition, 'Hell, Mark, I don't mean that I think you need them t—!'

'Why not?' the big cowhand interrupted, showing no offence. 'Because we could all sure use Dusty, 'specially, the way things stand here.'

Ever a realist and without an envious bone in his enormous frame, Mark was not ashamed to admit his limitations!

Before leaving Pegler's livery barn, the blond giant had been told by the doctor and the Humphrey brothers—none of whom had openly questioned the identity supplied to Gilmore and Stern—of what had happened during and after the thwarted attempt to hold up the Cattlemen's Bank. Combined with the comments he had heard when leaving the backhouse, and the attitude of his would be assailants, he had realized what he had come up against. From what he had been told, however—the reputation acquired by the Cousins' clan notwithstanding—the majority of the population would have been ready to defend the town providing they had a suitable leader.

Collier would have supplied the guidance, but was incapacitated!

Well liked and generally respected though Deputy Town Marshal Herman 'Pockets' Hoscroft might be, he could not fill the need!

Asked for the help he was supposed to supply as county

sheriff, Lloyd Bowman had claimed he could not spare deputies as there was a rumour the Smokey Hill Thompson gang were planning to raid the bank in Garnett. He had promised to fetch men if the rumours regarding Frank Cousins should prove correct, but everybody knew this would come too late to be of use. Nor, Dr. Connel and the Humphrey brothers had stated, was Lloyd Bowman sufficiently well liked by the population to have supplied the inducement and leadership to stand and fight, even if he was present.

Regardless of his competence, the blond giant was willing to concede he could not personally fill the bill, even if he announced his true identity!

Mark was well known as being a top hand at cattle work, for possessing enormous physical strength, and as a member of Ole Devil Hardin's floating outfit. For all that, he was aware that he lacked the well deserved reputation and personality which made his *amigo*, Captain Dustine Edward Marsden 'Dusty' Fog the kind of leader called for by the situation. The local cowhands would probably have considered him suitable in the absence of the Rio Hondo gun wizard, but they were too few in number to be of use. Given time, he felt sure he could win over sufficient of the citizens to form a fighting force capable of at least making Frank Cousins have second thoughts over tackling them.

Unfortunately, time was something unlikely to be granted!

'I haven't helped any by saying I was—!' the blond giant began, meaning to mention the alibi he had given and which he did not doubt would be exploited by the faction opposed to defiance when he told his real name.

'There's one thing might help you,' Collier put in, feeling his senses starting to spin and knowing the sedation was once more taking effect. 'I'm allowed by civic ordinance to appoint a temporary marshal to take over should I not be able to do it for any reason. The badge should help you.'

'It would at that!' Madam agreed, crossing quickly to the wardrobe. 'Do we need to get anybody else's permission, Tune?'

'Nope,' the peace officer replied, his voice becoming slurred, watching the blonde taking the badge of office from his vest. 'Just say, "I swear by Almighty God to do the duty of town marshal of Tennyson, Sand County, Texas, to the best of my ability", Mark, then pin on that old tin star.'

'Yo!' the big cowhand responded, with the traditional assent to an order of the United and Confederate States' cavalry.

Doing as he was requested, Mark saw his uncle lapse into unconsciousness before he could complete the oath of office, much less tell of the alias whereby he would have learnt Jessica and Trudeau Front de Boeuf were in town.

'You look like you could use some food and sleep,' Madam claimed, after having replaced the covers over the now motionless marshal with great gentleness.

'I didn't reckon it showed, ma'am,' Mark replied and, despite being eager to accept the suggestion, he went on, 'But I'd best go and meet up with Uncle Tune's deputy and make *habla* with Calam, her and me being good friends.'

'You'll be a whole heap more set to handle things *after* you've fed and had some rest,' the blonde contradicted in tones of determination. 'And, happen your Uncle Tune was awake, he'd tell you I'm one woman who's more than just tolerable set to having her own way when she puts her mind to anything.'

'Which being, ma'am,' the blond giant drawled, giving a gallant bow, 'I'll just natural' play things the way *you* want.' Knowing he had received good advice, he found himself thinking of how much alike the buxom woman and Calamity Jane were in many ways.

'Most folks come around to thinking that way after they've known me for a spell,' Madam claimed. 'You've just caught on faster than some.'

* * *

'Was he a friend of yours?' Mark Counter challenged, looking across the bar-room and twirling away his right hand

Colt 1860 Army Model revolver with a speed almost equal to that with which he had drawn it to defend himself from the hired killer who had deliberately provoked a quarrel with him.[1]

While enjoying the meal brought at her orders, Mark had had confirmed the story of the confrontations between Madam Bulldog and Calamity Jane. Much to his relief, he had discovered that the buxom blonde was far from feeling animosity towards the spunky girl with whom he enjoyed considerably more than just a platonic association. Rather she had shown signs of a liking and respect for the red head.

Telling how Calamity had explained her decision to remain in town, Madam admitted this had not as yet produced any unexpected information. Despite having spent much time in the small saloon owned by Rudolph Schanz, she had failed to obtain even a hint of there being an intention on the part of him and his cronies to offer active collaboration with Frank Cousins. She had merely confirmed the blonde's suspicions that they were responsible for the various rumours and alarms calculated to undermine any spirit of resistance if the outlaws should be coming.

Having slept for a few hours and woken refreshed, the blond giant had decided to go in search of his uncle's deputy and Calamity. While doing so, he would also allow himself to be seen around the town. Going downstairs, he had found a fair sized crowd present in the bar-room.

That there should be considerable interest displayed over his appearance, much of it having been directed at the badge of office pinned to the black leather vest he had donned, had come as no surprise to Mark. Knowing such smallish towns as Tennyson, he did not doubt that everybody was aware of his relationship with Marshal Tune Collier. Having just as certainly heard how he had dealt with Joshua Gilmore and

1. *Although we have discovered we were in error when suggesting Madam Bulldog participated in the incident, the confrontation between Mark Counter and the hired killer, Alvin Cordby, occurred in much the same fashion as we described in the narrative from which this book is an 'expansion'. J.T.E.*

Moses Stern on his arrival, probably the majority of them had been wondering whether he had merely adopted the name, 'Trudeau Front de Boeuf' and was really the man to whom the owner of the Hide And Horn Saloon had sent a request for assistance. If this should prove the case, they would also have been speculating over when they could expect Dusty Fog and the Ysabel Kid to come on the scene, as neither were as yet with him.

Crossing to the bar with the intention of asking for directions, the blond giant had seen the interest being taken in him by three men in particular. Before Alvin Cordby had walked over to provoke him into a gun fight, he had learned from a bartender that the other two were Rudolph Schanz and Wilbur Wardle, cronies of the blacksmith. Proving to be sufficiently fast on the draw, he had survived the attempt to kill him and had turned upon the pair he felt certain were responsible.

'We've never seen him afore he came in and sat at our table,' Schanz lied, thankful both that he had kept secret from all except his cronies the hiring of the killer, and that the killer had arrived separately at the saloon. 'That was real fancy shooting, mister, and you didn't have no choice over throwing down on him like you did. But how come you're wearing the marshal's badge?'

'Uncle Tune asked me to put it on, and swore me in, like he's allowed to when he can't handle things himself,' Mark replied, but once more decided against supplying his real name. 'And, so long as I'm wearing it, no lousy bunch of owlhoots are going to come shooting, looting and burning around this town.'

'You reckon you can stop 'em, Mr. *Front de Boeuf*?' Wardle challenged.

'This feller you and your *amigo*'d never seen before until he came to sit at your table might reckon I could make a damned good try at it,' the blond giant answered. 'But, happen you or anybody else thinks different, just stand up and say so.' Pausing for a few seconds, he went on when there was no response to his declaration, 'Well, that being the case, I'll go and make the rounds.'

Although he knew he had impressed the crowd, and news of the incident would be relayed quickly around the town, as he was leaving the bar-room, the blond giant realized he still had a long way to go before he won over the support of enough of the citizens to present a challenge likely to frighten off Frank Cousins' gang.

Or to stand a chance of fighting them off if they came!

CHAPTER FOURTEEN

It's For *Everybody's* Benefit

'Cousins will be here tonight,' Edward Kinsella announced, sinking with obvious exhaustion and relief into the most comfortable chair offered by the room into which he had just been admitted.

There was a haggard and dishevelled look about the generally neat 'travelling salesman'. This resulted from the unaccustomed amount of hard and fast travelling on horse-back to which he had been subjected over the past few days. It seemed to him that he had been almost constantly in the saddle, carrying messages between Jessica Front de Boeuf and Frank Cousins. Nor had his condition been improved as a result of the Front de Boeufs being confined to the Fortescue Hotel since the arrival of Mark Counter. It was imperative that Counter remained in ignorance of the presence of Jessica and her son and she had demanded the solace of sexual intercourse every time Kinsella had returned to report developments.

On reaching Purdey's trading post to deliver news of the thwarted hold up, Kinsella had found the confidence of the beautiful woman justified. As she had anticipated, Cousins was there accompanied by several of his men. In one respect, the haste with which the 'salesman' had travelled had proved unnecessary as the outlaw leader had already heard what had happened. Not from the pair who had escaped, however, neither of them being willing to seek him out. Having had similar designs upon the Cattlemen's Bank to those of his dead nephew, the news had been brought by a man he had sent to carry out a reconnaissance for him.

However, Kinsella had discovered that the outlaw leader was disinclined to take punitive action, due to a wish to avoid arousing further protests while he was uncertain of how effective the soon to be elected replacement for the Reconstruction Administration might prove themselves to be. Kinsella had therefore used the arguments supplied by Jessica to show the disadvantages of not taking action. Despite conceding to refrain might induce witnesses from Benson City to testify before a Grand Jury, Cousins had pointed out there was no certainty that one would be convened. Furthermore, as he had believed he was attending a peace meeting with Smokey Hill Thompson, he had only brought a few of his men with him. It would, he had claimed, be impossible to gather sufficient reinforcements in the short time available before the commencement of the campaigns to win votes launched by those seeking election. Once this began, it would be highly inadvisable to carry out an act so likely to be seized upon and used by candidates as a means of acquiring support from the voters. Nor—despite believing they might be able to settle their differences amicably—would he be able to enlist assistance from Thompson, who had frequently expressed criticism of his 'cut one, they all bleed' activities in the past.

Accepting the validity of both arguments (he had anticipated something of the sort might be presented) Kinsella had countered them with an inducement suggested by his investigations in Tennyson. He had asserted there was a stronger majority amongst the population than was in fact the case, who would be willing to overlook an act of vengeance, providing it was only inflicted upon the two people directly responsible for killing Brock Cousins. Promising to act as a go-between from the gang leader to the town, he had won a somewhat grudging agreement that punitive action would be taken against Madam Bulldog and Marshal Tune Collier.

The intervening time had been spent by Kinsella in what a later generation might have called 'commuting' from Tennyson to the trading post, although with a less innocent purpose than implied by the word. It had proved to be an exhausting process. Not only had he to report on developments in town to Cousins, but he had also to alternate between satisfying Jessica's boredom—induced lust and guiding the thinking of the faction led by Joshua Gilmore. As the result of the latter, Calamity Jane had been unable to win the confidence of that group. Although Gilmore's group had not known of her association with Mark Counter, the Front de Boeufs, having kept in touch with his activities, were better informed. When Gilmore's gang had been told of the friendship between Counter and Calamity, possessing distrustful natures they had been wary where she was concerned, even before the arrival of the blonde giant. Even though she and the Texan were not seen to make contact with one another (in fact she had spoken in a derogatory fashion about him and implied they were no longer on speaking terms) they had remained unconvinced and refused to allow her to share their intentions.

Returning shortly before noon of the seventh day after the hold up, Kinsella found Jessica in her room and clad in a scanty fashion. However he was relieved by the presence of Trudeau Front de Boeuf in her room. Hoping this would prevent him from being expected to join her in bed when he had finished his report, he had told them what he had discovered.

'What time will they be here?' the woman asked, making no attempt to close the flimsy robe which was almost all she was wearing.

'As soon as I let him know Gilmore's crowd are ready to back him,' the "salesman" replied, more worried than stimulated by the state of semi-nudity with which he was confronted.

'They won't do anything like that openly,' Front de Boeuf claimed. 'The best he can expect from them is they will stay well out of his way.'

'Then he won't come!' Kinsella stated. 'He's only got a dozen men and says that isn't enough without he has their help.'

'In which case,' Jessica said with grim finality. 'He's going to *have* their help!'

'But they won't—!' the massive young man began.

'They won't help him by going to the Hide And Horn Saloon while he's having Madam Bulldog and Tune Collier shot down, much less take part in the shooting themselves,' the woman admitted shortly, never caring to be interrupted. 'But, not knowing how few men he has, they'll be willing to save themselves and their property by making sure nobody else stands by Bulldog and Collier.'

'How do you mean?' Kinsella asked.

'They'll be satisfied they're acting in a way which will appear it is for the benefit of the town as a whole,' Jessica replied and explained what she had in mind.

'By god, *yes!*' the "salesman" ejaculated in admiration, when the woman stopped speaking. 'They'll chance going *that* far, if it's put to them properly. And, when he hears what they've done, Cousins won't be able to refuse to come in after Bulldog and Collier.'

'There's only one thing wrong, though, momma,' Front de Boeuf objected. 'If it works, how will we be able to have Cousin Mark killed?'

'Either you or Edward will do it,' Jessica replied. 'No matter which it is, the blame will be put on Cousins and his men.'

'Sure it will,' Kinsella agreed, then reached into the side pocket of his jacket. 'I almost forgot, Jess', but this was at Purdey's for you.'

Taking the crumpled and grubby envelope she was offered, the woman gave a disinterested sniff. She recognized the writing of the address and knew it had been passed along the line of communication she had established to help her keep in touch with matters of importance. However, the only correspondence recently from the man responsible for the letter had been increasing demands for payment to be sent in recompense for his services.

'I'll read it later!' the woman decided after a moment, tossing the envelope unopened on to the dressing-table.

Glancing at her son, she continued, 'Why don't you go and play patience in your room, dear?'

'I'd best go and start talking Gilmore and his crowd into doing what we want,' Kinsella said hurriedly, reaching for his hat and starting towards the door, before Front de Boeuf could reply.

* * *

'Stay put and let that rig fall!'

Having started to turn on realizing the door of her room had been unlocked and thrown open, even although she had not heard her key pushed out onto the thick carpet,[1] Calamity Jane realized she could do nothing except obey.

'If this's a hold up, you've picked the wr—!' the red head began, recognizing the intruders as Moses Stern and Wilbur Wardle, despite the hoods made from flour sacks they were wearing. She was conscious that she was in no position to do anything other than obey.

'It isn't!' the storekeeper interrupted. 'We're members of the Tennyson Regulators!'

'What the hell'd they be?' the red head demanded, standing very still and allowing the gunbelt she had been about to strap on to drop to the floor behind her.

'Folks who don't aim to see this town treated like Benson City,' Wardle explained, wanting to establish the "honourable" motives of himself and his cronies. 'Seeing's how Madam Bulldog's got her a tame marshal and won't listen to reason, we've appointed ourselves to make her change her mind. It's for *everybody's* benefit!'

Always a persuasive talker, Edward Kinsella had had little difficulty in winning acceptance when suggesting Jessica Front de Boeuf's scheme to Joshua Gilmore's faction. There

---

1. *An occasion when the life of Calamity Jane was saved by having heard the key to her door dropping to the floor after having been pushed from its hole by an intruder is described in:* WHITE STALLION, RED MARE. *J.T.E.*

had only been one major objection, but he had explained it away. Having learned the true identity of Mark Counter the previous day, they had been concerned about the possibility of reprisals from that direction after their work was done. The 'salesman' had satisfied them this would not prove to be the case. With Collier dead, they could appoint one of their number to take over as marshal and local deputy for Sheriff Lloyd Bowman, who they knew would give them backing. With an elected Administration being so close to becoming a fact, chiefly as a result of General Jackson Baines 'Ole Devil' Hardin's efforts, no man employed by him would endanger this by taking drastic and, ostensibly, illegal measures against a peace officer. Having had that point settled to their satisfaction, and believing they would emerge with credit for having saved the town from being ravaged by Frank Cousins and his outlaws, they had considered they had the solution to all their problems. Nor, despite generally being distrustful, had they questioned the claim made by the 'salesman' that he was being forced to act as intermediary due to Cousins having taken his wife hostage.

Shortly after night had fallen, the party had set out to put the plan into operation. Much to the disappointment of the watching Kinsella, their visit to the jailhouse had not resulted in the shooting of Mark Counter, thereby saving him from possibly having to kill the blond giant. Waiting until satisfied that the blond giant and Deputy Town Marshal Herman 'Pockets' Hoscroft were secured in a cell, later to be joined by Madam Bulldog's employees under the inducement of Joseph Turner's wife and young child being held as hostage, the 'salesman' had set off to tell Cousins—who was hiding two miles outside the town—that the raid upon the Hide And Horn Saloon could take place as arranged earlier in the afternoon.

Although Calamity had been at Schanz's saloon during the afternoon, he and his cronies had been so cautious that she had not realized anything was in the wind. Returning to her room at the Fortescue Hotel, after having visited Pegler's livery barn in the hope of finding Mark there and to attend to her buckskin stallion, she had decided to try some other means of making contact with him. Changing clothes before setting out, she was caught in a difficult position by the intruders. She had thrown off the effects of the only fight she had ever lost, due in part to the ministrations secretly administered by Madam Bulldog's maid, but she was unable to respond as she wished while holding her gunbelt in both hands and being covered by two revolvers.

'I'm all for folks's thinks of others,' the red head asserted, with an even tone which suggesting nothing of the anxiety she was experiencing. 'Let's hope Mark Counter and that fat old bitch from the Hide And Horn see it that way.'

'They will,' Wardle declared and continued, trying to sound sincere, 'Now us Regulators've got everybody who'd've stood by her corralled with Counter and Pockets Hoscroft at the jailhouse, we're going to leave a buckboard outside the Hide And Horn for her to take Tune Collier to Garnett, where he'll be safe enough under Sheriff Bowman's protection, afore Frank Cousins and his gang get here.'

'She struck me's being a mighty stubborn old bitch,' Calamity claimed, struggling inwardly to prevent an increasing rage bursting from her. She knew an appearance of passive acceptance of the situation was required. 'What if she won't use it?'

'Then, no matter what happens, it's all *her* doing and none of ours,' the storekeeper answered. 'We're doing all we can to protect the town as a whole and still give her a chance to save herself and Collier.'

'Come on, Wilb'!' Stern growled impatiently, 'Let's get done what we come for and get the hell out of it.'

'Are you leaving me *here*?' Calamity asked, with well simulated alarm.

'We ain't taking you with us, that's for sure!' Stern declared, his ego still smarting from the memory of the treatment he had received at the hands of the red head on their first meeting.

'Oh my good God!' Calamity gasped, still calling upon all

159

her skill as a poker player to produce the desired effect. 'Can't *one* of you stay with me?'

'Why?' Wardle wanted to know, concluding, as she had intended, that the request had been directed at him and not his companion.

'Cousins might've sent word that he'd come in peaceable, should he be given a clear run at Bulldog and the marshal,' the red head explained, eyeing the storekeeper with what she hoped would be taken for a mixture of pleading and the suggestion of a worthwhile recompense. Glancing pointedly at the bed, she went on, 'But I'd feel a whole heap happier and safer happen I'd got one of the Tennyson Regulators here to tell any owlhoots that happened by's I'm in his protection.'

'You would at that,' Wardle answered with enthusiasm, running a lasciviously appreciative gaze over the very shapely figure of the girl and thinking that, as neither he nor any of his cronies believed the presentation of the buckboard would help keep alive the objects of Cousins' wrath, it could prove advantageous to have the cast-iron alibi of being with Calamity Jane when their killing was investigated. 'In that case, I reckon it's only right I take care of you myself. You go tell Josh and the boys what I'm doing, Moe.'

'How about that sick dude and his mother?' Stern inquired, the son having supposedly contracted a severe attack of the grippe which had been the Front de Boeufs' excuse for remaining in their rooms since the arrival of their intended victim.

'Go tell them to keep off the street, no matter what they hear,' the storekeeper replied. 'Happen you're lucky, that right handsome widow-woman might ask if you'll protect her like I'm going to do Calam.'

'Sure,' Stern growled, with a complete lack of hope, and turned reluctantly to leave.

'Well now,' Wardle said, after the door had closed behind his departing companion. 'He's gone and that leaves only you and me.'

'Like you say, he's gone and that leaves only you and me,'

160

Calamity replied. 'Only, way you've acted towards me since I've been in town, I didn't reckon you liked me.'

'It wasn't *that*!' the storekeeper asserted, returning his revolver to its holster. 'I'd heard's how you and Mark Counter were sort of—*friendly*—and didn't reckon you'd want anybody else cutting in.'

'We was more than just god-damned *friendly*!' the red head declared, sounding indignant. 'Fact being, time was I reckoned I could quit working my butt off driving a freight wagon to live all fat and comfortable as the very rich Mrs. Mark Counter, but he got tied in with that hot-assed she-male owlhoot, Belle Starr, and dropped me flat.'

There was such apparent animosity in the girl's voice, she might have been serious in her complaint. In fact, she had spoken a certain amount of truth. But regardless of her frequently intimate association with the blond giant, at no time had the possibility of marriage ever entered her head. Nor, although she was aware that he had developed very strong feelings for Belle Starr, had she ever regarded this with a sense of betrayal. Always a realist, she had considered —no matter that the other was a known outlaw—that Belle and Mark were far more suited for matrimony than she and the blond giant would ever be.

'The dirty dog!' Wardle said, with what he hoped sounded sincerity. He removed his hood and continued, 'If there's one thing riles me, it's a man who does a woman wrong.'

'*You* wouldn't do it, I can tell,' Calamity claimed, stepping forward to place her hands behind the neck of the smirking storekeeper.

'Would I he—!' Wardle commenced.

Powered by an exceptionally well muscled right leg, the knee which passed between the thighs of the storekeeper brought the declaration to an abrupt end. Taken in the most vulnerable portion of the masculine anatomy with a far from gentle impact, the sudden and completely unexpected agony rendered him incapable of conscious thought or actions. Torment and nausea caused him to stumble away from the girl and double at the waist. Before he could get far enough away to save himself, she jerked downwards with her hands, and increased the folding motion so she could continue the attack. Bringing up and bending her right leg, she propelled its knee violently against his descending face. Blood sprayed from his crushed and, as it was discovered later, badly broken nose. The hands left his neck and he was thrown over to alight upon his back. In doing so, his head struck the floor with sufficient force to completely render him unconscious.

Bending to snatch the ivory handled Colt Navy Model of 1853 revolver from her gunbelt, Calamity darted to the door. Easing it open, she looked cautiously along the passage. Showing no sign of having heard what had happened to his companion, Stern was being admitted by the massive young man into the room of the woman she had learned had signed the register as 'Mrs. Jessica Cholmondeley'.

'All right, you lousy son-of-a-bitch!' the red head hissed at her unheeding victim, having returned to retrieve and buckle on her gunbelt. 'I'm going to help Madam and Mark. But, should they get made wolf bait and I come through, I'll be back to finish you off the slowest way I can figure!'

* * *

'Well, momma,' Trudeau Front de Boeuf said with satisfaction, after the instructions had been given to Moses Stern and he had withdrawn. 'It's going as we want!'

'So it would seem,' the beautiful woman replied, but with less enthusiasm.

Much to her annoyance, Jessica Front de Boeuf had not been able to sate her passion at the expense of Edward Kinsella during the afternoon. He had, she suspected, deliberately avoided having to remain in her company for long enough to play his part. Instead, she had been compelled to pass the time practising various tricks of crooked gamblers with her son. To give her credit, such was her strength of will, she had been able to concentrate upon the demanding tasks of shuffling a deck until it was in a pre-determined

162

'sequence, nullifying a cut which would otherwise have changed this, and dealing the second or some other card without detection instead of the one on top.[2]

From sundown, the Front de Boeufs had kept watch upon the Square from the window of her room. Like Kinsella, they had been disappointed when there was no shooting from the jailhouse. However, being aware of how competent her nephew was as a gun fighter, Jessica had admitted she was not confident in the ability of the 'Tennyson Regulators' to achieve what was required. It would, she had stated, be much more reliable for Kinsella to shoot him and the elderly deputy town marshal through the bars of the cell after they had been disarmed and locked in.

'Can we rely on Cousins to keep his men in check, momma?' Front de Boeuf inquired.

'This isn't like Benson City. Instead of having the whole town suffer all he wants to do here is show he's not afraid to take revenge on the pair who killed his nephew,' Jessica replied. 'But I think I'll get my Derringer, just in case some of his men might not be satisfied with the loot from the saloon and come looking for more.'

'That would be as well,' the massive young man agreed.

'Good heavens!' the woman ejaculated, on crossing to the dressing-table. 'Here's that letter from Turnbull. I'd forgotten all about it.'

'You'd best see what he has to say,' Front de Boeuf suggested. 'It might be something important.'

'More likely it's only another of his whining demands for money,' Jessica sniffed, but she tore open the envelope and, extracting a sheet of paper, began to read.

'What is it, momma!' Front de Boeuf asked, seeing the woman stiffen and an expression of alarm come to her beautiful face.

'W—We can't let Mark Counter be killed!' Jessica replied in a strangled voice.

2. *The definitive volume describing how such dishonest gambling techniques are carried out is:* SCARNE ON CARDS, *by John Scarne. J.T.E.*

'Why not?' the young man wanted to know.

'Turnbull has heard what's in Aunt Cornelia's will,' the woman explained, her hands shaking with emotion. 'She is leaving all her money to Mark, as she threatened. But she claims she is so certain of his complete honesty that, only if he should be killed as a result of committing any kind of crime, can it all come to us.'

'Good God!' Front de Boeuf gasped. 'That means—!'

'Yes,' Jessica finished bitterly, thinking of all the hours and money they had spent bringing their scheme to fruition. 'It means if he dies tonight, we won't get a thin dime!'

CHAPTER FIFTEEN

We've Had To Change The Plan

'If you can get to the saloon and tell Madam Bulldog help is on the way, Miss Calamity,' Trudeau Front de Boeuf suggested, as his mother, the girl and he came together in the second floor passage of the Fortescue Hotel, 'Momma and I will go and help Cousin Mark to escape from the jailhouse.'

'I'll get to her,' Calamity Jane promised. 'And God help anybody who tries to stop me doing it!'

'If anybody should try, make sure you deal with them silently,' Jessica Front de Boeuf advised in her usual haughty fashion. 'I don't think we can cope with both Cousins and his men and those "Tennyson Regulators", or whatever they call themselves, at the same time.'

'I'll keep it in mind,' the red head promised, just a trifle annoyed by the attitude of the beautiful woman. Making a gesture with the Winchester Model of 1866 carbine she was carrying to augment her Colt Navy Model of 1853 revolver and bull whip, she went on, 'I'll whomp 'em with the butt of this. But are you sure you want to come along with us?'

'Cousin Tune and Nephew Mark are in trouble,' Jessica replied, with what appeared to be genuine sincerity. 'And our family are like that of Cousins in one respect. If you cut one of us, the rest bleed. So it is my duty to do all I can to help them. Now, we'd best be moving before it's too late.'

Having armed herself fully, ready to embark upon a rescue mission, Calamity had been surprised by a knock on her door. Entering the room, the massive young man had

165

introduced himself as Mark Counter's cousin and suggested co-operation. He had explained that he and his mother were using the name, 'Cholmondeley' to avoid embarassing Town Marshal Tune Collier by letting it be known he was related to a professional gambler, and that he had pretended to be suffering from the grippe so as to offer an excuse for them to remain in case their wounded kinsman needed help. Satisfied by his explanations, the red head had agreed to co-operate in helping to deal with the problem.

Waiting for Front de Boeuf to join her in the passage, Calamity had been surprised when he had arrived accompanied by his mother. Despite wondering what had induced the beautiful and arrogant woman to take part in such a dangerous and unladylike expedition, she had been willing to concede both were dressed in a manner that was suitable for the action that was planned.

The young man had changed into a dark shirt and trousers and was bare-headed. In addition to carrying his Greener whipit gun, he had the Colt 1860 Army Model revolver from his 'Grizzly Bear' disguise, and his Colt Pocket Pistol of Navy calibre thrust butt forward into each side of his waist band. Although she knew nothing of him and his activities, her instincts warned he was less the soft and pampered 'momma's boy' than appeared on the surface, and she was confident the weapons were for more than just a bluff.

For her part, having discarded her stylish garments, Jessica had stuffed her hair under her son's white 'planter's' hat. An open black cloak hung over the kind of black sleeveless bodice and tights used by ballet dancers when practising and there were flat heeled pumps on her feet. Counting upon everybody being too engrossed in what was to take place to think about the kind of weapon with which the marshal had been wounded, she had elected to bring the Winchester rifle she could use so effectively as well as her Remington Double Derringer. However, being just as unaware of her true nature and potential, the red head wondered whether she might not

166

prove more of a liability than an asset in the trouble which was sure to be forthcoming.

Realizing there was nothing to be gained and much to be lost if she allowed her resentment over the somewhat condescending manner of the woman to cloud her judgement, Calamity nodded at her explanation and started to lead the way to the stairs.

'Hold it!' the red head whispered urgently, waving her companions back with the carbine as she was nearing the stairhead. 'Somebody's coming!'

As she delivered the warning, Calamity whipped off her battered U.S. cavalry kepi and peered with the minimum of exposure around the edge of the wall. Identifying the still hooded man who was ascending, the revolver now tucked into his waist band, she withdrew her head. He had been looking downwards in his usual shambling fashion and she was confident that she had avoided detection.

'Who is it?' Front de Boeuf whispered.

'Moe Stern,' the red head replied. 'The jasper who—!'

'Take this, Tru!' Jessica commanded, speaking just as quietly as the other two and holding out her rifle. 'Leave him to *me*!'

'Yes, momma,' the massive young man assented, having none of the doubts which were assailing the girl over the suggestion.

Relieved of the Winchester and leaving the little twin-barrelled pistol in the pocket of her tights, Jessica walked forward with a heavier step than was necessary. Hearing her, as she had intended, Moses Stern raised his head and his right hand went towards the butt of his revolver. He made no attempt to draw it. Instead, he stared with lecherous delight at the eye-catching sight presented by the beautiful and extremely curvaceous woman. She halted with arms akimbo, spreading further apart the cloak to exhibit all the better the contours of her body which was encased in garments fitting as snugly as a second skin and with a decollete which left no doubt the bodice alone covered her imposing and thrust forward bosom.

167

'I've been pulling on the bell-rope until my arm aches, but nobody has come up to answer!' Jessica announced, such a device having been installed in the hotel since the class of guests had improved and such a servive had become expected. Her manner was haughty and complaining as she spoke. 'Aren't there any of the staff downstairs, my good man?'

'Nope,' Stern replied, resuming his briefly interrupted ascent. 'We telled 'em to go home and keep offen Frank Cousins' trail, so that's what they've done.'

'Are you here alone?'

'Wilb' Wardle's up there with Calamity Jane, but I'm on my lonesome down he—!'

'Then who is *that?*' Jessica demanded, staring with well simulated horror down the stairs.

Startled by the way in which the question was put, and with his normally suspicious nature distracted due to the appearance presented by the woman, the thought that he was being subjected to an ancient ploy never entered Stern's head. Once more reaching for his revolver, he began to swing around so as to investigate. Instantly, Jessica raised her shapely and firm muscled left leg to kick him hard between the shoulders. Already off balance, his head struck the wall as he was precipitated downwards. Continuing his uncontrolled descent, there was an audible crack of bone breaking when he crashed to the floor of the entrance lobby.

Showing a speed which came as something of a surprise to Calamity, despite her belief that he would prove beneficial to the rescue bid, Front de Boeuf moved forward. Handing the Winchester to his mother in passing, he darted downstairs.

'It's all right!' the young man reported, having disappeared briefly while making an investigation. 'The front door is closed and I couldn't see any sign of him having been heard as he hit the floor.'

'I'd say he's bust his neck,' Calamity remarked, having descended with Jessica, and glancing at the sprawled out, unmoving figure of the burly man.

'I won't lose any sleep over that,' the woman declared, her manner calmly disinterested. 'Will you?'

'Can't say I will,' the red head confessed, studying the speaker in a fresh light. Realizing there were hard muscles under the seemingly soft and pampered exterior, she put the matter from her mind and went on, 'What's doing outside, friend?'

'They've left the buckboard hitched outside the saloon,' Front de Boeuf reported, amused by the change he sensed in the demeanour of the girl so far as his mother was concerned. Being aware of how capably she could defend herself physically when the need arose, he had not been in the least surprised by her handling of the potential threat to their mission.[1] 'None of them are with it, but two are on the sidewalk outside the jailhouse.'

'There is no sign of Cousins, I suppose?' Jessica asked, although the timbre of her words was more in the nature of a statement.

'None, momma,' Front de Boeuf confirmed. 'But I should think they will soon be arriving.'

'Then we'd best get moving!' Calamity stated.

'How are you going to reach the saloon?' Jessica inquired.

'Go out the back and up to cross where the street narrows,' the red head replied. 'I don't reckon those yahoos would figure out what I'm aiming to do, but I'm not about to chance having to talk them into letting me by.'

'I think you're wise,' the woman admitted and started to lead the way towards the rear of the lobby. 'We'll have to go the same kind of route, but in the opposite direction, as that will improve all our chances of getting across the street.'

'Let's hope we're all in time!' Calamity said grimly, now confident that Jessica would prove of value to their endeavour.

'What a coarse creature!' the beautiful woman asserted,

---

1. *An example of how effective Jessica Front de Boeuf could be when in a physical confrontation with another woman is described in:* Part Four, 'Another Type Of Badger Game', WANTED, BELLE STARR! *J.T.E.*

watching the red head hurrying away after they had left through the kitchen door without being challenged.

'Yes, momma,' Front de Boeuf replied, long experience having taught him this was the easiest response when wishing to avoid a discussion or argument, although he had found the girl easy on the eye and liked her independent spirit.

Going in the opposite direction to Calamity, the woman and the young man listened for any indication of her having run into difficulties. They also kept a careful watch to avoid being seen, thus having to deal with anybody wishing to question their activities. Neither eventuality materialized and soon they were passing the last building on their side of the Square and were faced with crossing the narrower portion of Vernon Street. Continuing along until another building lay behind them, this was accomplished without difficulty and, as no alarm was raised from the other end of the Square, they assumed the girl had been equally successful in avoiding detection.

Passing through an alley, the Front de Boeufs found the quarter moon was giving sufficient light for them to see their destination. As they walked towards it, they could hear several horses approaching from beyond the Square. Before either could comment upon the implications of the sound, Edward Kinsella stepped out having been lurking in the shadows of the building they were passing while waiting to carry out his instructions.

'What's happened?' the "travelling salesman" demanded, although he was now dressed after the fashion of a cowhand, his orders being to go and kill Mark Counter as soon as he heard shots from the Hide And Horn Saloon.

'We've had to change the plan!' Jessica replied. 'There's no need for you to shoot young Counter and the deputy after Cousins gets here, but you'd better go and get your horse ready to leave town.'

'Whatever you say,' Kinsella assented and, despite wondering what had caused the alteration to the arrangements, he made no attempt to satisfy his curiosity. 'It would have been easy enough, though. With all the people Gilmore and his bunch have brought and put in the cells, there'd have been plenty of witnesses willing to put the blame on Cousins' men.'

'Which cell is he in?' the woman snapped, not caring to be reminded of the time, effort and money expended upon the now abortive scheme.

'That o——!' Kinsella began, pointing. 'What the——?'

Having turned their attention in the direction indicated, the Front de Boeufs were just as startled as he was by the sight which met their gaze!

Much to the amazement of the onlookers, the set of bars in question were suddenly wrenched inwards from their setting in the back wall of the jailhouse!

'It must be Cousin Mark!' Front de Boeuf guessed accurately, remembering the tremendous strength of his kinsman even when they were children.

Even while delivering the pronouncement, the massive young man realized his cousin had created danger by seeking to escape in such a fashion. The sound of the bars being forcibly removed had reached the ears of the men in front of the building. Giving profane exclamations of alarm, instead of going through the office to reach the cells, they began to run along the alley.

Waiting until the pair had almost reached the end, Front de Boeuf stepped out to confront them. Before either could react to his unexpected appearance, he went into action with devastating speed. Swinging the whipit gun around and up with his right hand, he proved it to be as effective as a club as it was when used in its intended capacity of firearm. Caught at the side of his hooded head, Joshua Gilmore was spun in one direction. An instant later, reversing their course before any defensive measures could even be contemplated much less put into effect, the short twin barrels delivered a similar blow to Rudolph Schanz. Also the recipient of what later proved to be a fractured skull, from which neither ever fully recovered, he went the other way to his stricken companion.

'That's settled them!' Jessica declared with satisfaction, unperturbed by the thought that her son might have killed two ostensibly honest and law-abiding, if misguided, citizens. 'You'd better leave, Edward. If I know young Counter, he'll be bound and determined to go and rescue Collier and that woman at the saloon.'

'Sure, Jess',' the "travelling salesman" agreed, equally aware of the inadvisability of his remaining where he might be seen and his participation in the affair made public. 'Shall I meet you at Purdey's?'

'Make it Fort Worth,' the woman decided. 'Should Cousins survive and escape, we had better keep out of his way until I can smooth things out with him.'

'I'd best go and offer to help Cousin Mark,' Front de Boeuf offered, seeing the blond giant was starting to climb through the space created by the removal of the bars. 'It won't do for him to be killed, would it?'

'*No,*' Jessica confirmed. 'But I'll be easier in my mind if Cousins and any of the others who might guess something of what's happened don't survive to talk about it.'

Strange as it might seem, while he had been willing to have let the original scheme reach its required conclusion, Front de Boeuf was not entirely sorry the need to have his cousin killed no longer existed. Of all the family, only Mark had ever treated him as an equal, and at no time had he ever referred to him by the hated sobriquet, 'Cyrus'. Therefore, even without the inducement of the terms set out in Aunt Cornelia's will, he was not averse to helping the blond giant in whatever fighting lay ahead.

CHAPTER SIXTEEN

Nobody Kills Her But Me

Listening to the horses being brought to a halt outside the Hide And Horn Saloon, Madam Bulldog knew she would soon be facing her destiny.

On being informed that Mark Counter and Deputy Town Marshal Herman 'Pockets' Hoscroft had been taken prisoner, Joseph Turner was the first to offer a refusal to the demands made by Joshua Gilmore, regardless of the threat to his family. But the buxom blonde, knowing that to do otherwise would result in bloodshed, without preventing the arrival of Frank Cousins and his gang and further deaths in the ensuing fighting, had insisted upon everybody doing as they were ordered. There had nearly been a mutiny, but at last she was obeyed. Despite realizing that it would be of no avail to do so, she had promised that she and Town Marshal Tune Collier would seek to escape in the buckboard provided by the Tennyson Regulators. She had also pretended to accept the promise from the blacksmith that he and his men would return to help load the wounded peace officer as soon as those of her supporters likely to lead resistance were locked in the jailhouse.

Left alone in the bar-room, Madam had made what few preparations she could think of to offer some slight chance of salvation for Collier and herself. As she was dressed in one of the revealing gowns that she wore on the premises, she had discarded the shoulder holster. Instead, she was carrying the Webley Bulldog revolver in the fast draw rig of the gunbelt with which she had acquired a well deserved reputation for speed and accuracy in numerous exhibitions against targets. Aware that she could use the weapon to lethal effect when necessary, she hoped to at least be given a chance to go out fighting. Knowing that to have her sawed-off shotgun available would result in her being shot on sight, she had taken it from beneath the counter and given it to the marshal, who was able to sit up and hold it although he still was unable to stand or walk.

Having done all she could, the blonde had waited for the outlaws to arrive. There was, she had told herself, just one slender chance of survival. If she could convince Cousins that she was running the saloon on behalf of Rameses 'Ram' Turtle, he might be willing to save face by taking the considerable amount of money she kept in the safe in her private office and leave without harming either Collier or herself. To achieve such an end would call for a masterly bluff, but she believed herself a sufficiently accomplished poker player to at least make the attempt with some slight hope of success.

Footsteps crossed the sidewalk and hard faced, well armed men came warily through the front entrance. Having satisfied themselves that Madam was alone, they moved aside to let their leader and his brother enter. Tallish, fairly heavy in build, going bald and bespectacled, Frank Cousins had an aura of arrogance and looked more like a humourless politician of 'liberal' pretensions than the leader of a bloodthirsty outlaw gang. To his left, the father of the young man responsible for their presence was portly, more pompous in appearance, and yet ill at ease despite wearing an unaccustomed gunbelt. Of the other nine men who had preceded them into the bar-room—two having been left outside to keep watch—four were members of the clan and were better dressed in cowhand style and meaner looking than the others.

'Good evening, gentlemen,' Madam greeted, with what seemed an icy calm. 'I'm sorry for what happened to young Cousins, but he brought it upon himself.'

174

'God!' the leader of the gang growled. 'Isn't she the cool one, Brother Mort?'

'Yes,' Mortimer Cousins agreed, his instincts as a lawyer disturbed by the way in which the blonde was behaving.

'I know why you're here, Frank Cousins,' Madam claimed. 'But, before you do something you could have cause to *regret*, I must warn you that Ram Turtle isn't going to take kindly to it should you go ahead.'

'*Ram Turtle*?' the man to whom the warning was directed spat out. 'What the hell's he got to do with it?'

'This is *his* place,' the blonde explained, with such confidence she might have spoken the truth. 'Or did you think I could have afforded to buy it myself?'

'I heard's how she'd won it offen Maxie Higgins, boss!' one of the outlaws stated.

'So did I!' Cousins admitted pensively. 'And the Ram allus passes word when he's got somebody running a place for him, so's there's no fuss in it and it doesn't get busted up.'

'Maybe you hadn't got the word,' Madam suggested, deciding she was unlikely to achieve her purpose but determined to continue her bluff to the end.

'And maybe you're trying to run a bluff to save your hide!' the leader countered. 'If it was like you said, you'd have let the Ram know what was doing and he'd've warned me off. Sam, take one of the men and fetch that god-damned john-law son-of-a-bitch down here so we can hand him his needings.'

'You'll have to carry him,' Madam asserted truthfully, but continued with less veracity. 'He's still unconscious!'

'That's too bad,' Cousins sniffed. 'I was wanting him to know what was happening. Go see happen you can bring him 'round, Sam. Fetch him here if you can. If not, finish him off up there.'

'And what do you have in mind for me?' the blonde inquired as the two men were going upstairs. She was aware that Collier was not only conscious but armed and ready to shoot anybody who entered the bedroom unannounced.

175

'We're going to kill you for what you did to young Brock when you knew who he was,' Cousins replied, but was not permitted to say this would happen after the woman had been raped by any of the gang who felt so inclined.

'Like hell you are!' declared a feminine voice.

'What the hell?' Cousins snarled, glaring at the red haired girl in male clothing who came through the door leading to the kitchen at the rear of the saloon.

'The name's Calamity Jane,' the newcomer announced, making sure her hands stayed well away from the holstered Colt Navy Model of 1853 revolver and bull whip she was wearing. 'And, after what she had done to me, nobody kills her but me!'

Having seen what was happening at the jailhouse, while making her way towards the saloon, the red head had decided upon a course of action. Finding the door of the kitchen was not fastened, she had been able to gain admittance without needing to risk being heard forcing an entrance. Arriving as the outlaws were about to enter, she had listened to what was being said. When it was obvious the bluff made by Madam Bulldog would not succeed, she had prepared to put her own scheme into operation. Aware that to make her appearance carrying the Winchester Model of 1866 carbine might cause her to be shot before she could speak, she had left it behind.

'What did she do to you?' Mortimer Cousins inquired.

'Took me on in a fist fight and, when I was starting to whip her good, had her tail-peddling calico cats hold me while she pounded all hell out of me,' Calamity replied. 'I've been waiting until I was over what she done to come and call her down. Which I'm not about to let *anybody* stop me doing it.'

'You mean you want to draw down on her, woman to woman?' the lawyer suggested hopefully.

'That's what I've come here to do,' the red head affirmed.

'Do you reckon you can take her?' Mortimer Cousins asked.

'I *know* god-damned well I can!' Calamity stated with confidence.

'Then I feel you have the right to be given the opportunity

to do so,' the lawyer declared in his most judicious fashion. 'Don't you, Brother Frank?'

Despite his son having been the cause, Mortimer Cousins had never considered that demonstrating the 'cut one, they all bleed' principle was advisable under the prevailing conditions. They might be able to get away with a claim that the marshal was killed in self defence when he attacked them in a delirium caused by the drugs he had received as part of his treatment. However, for them to rape and murder a woman —even one unlikely to qualify as 'good', due to her being the owner of a saloon—was sure to raise a public outcry at a time when this kind of publicity should be avoided at all costs.

Now the lawyer believed there was a way out of the potentially dangerous situation. Less protest was likely to be forthcoming if the blonde was to meet her death at the hands of the vengeance seeking and famous Calamity Jane. She could offer a better and more acceptable motive than a desire to avenge an outlaw shot down in the commission of a crime. Therefore, he hoped his brother would accept his guidance and give an answer in the affirmative.

'All right,' the leader agreed, seeing the other members of the gang were eager to witness the confrontation and not averse to the prospect himself. 'She's all your'n, Calamity Jane.'

'Count up to five,' the red head requested, strolling forward until coming to a halt about ten feet from where Madam Bulldog was standing in front of the bar. 'When you get there, I'm starting to throw lead, regardless of what she does!'

'You heard her, blondie,' Cousins said, grinning evilly at the buxom woman. 'How do *you* feel about it?'

'She's a liar when she says I had her held, I didn't need to, she was so easy to take,' Madam replied, turning to face the red head and raising her right hand until it hovered over the butt of the Webley. 'Start your count and, no matter what *you* do to me after, she's going to be too dead to know about it.'

Listening to what was said, Calamity was delighted by the success of her scheme. However, when she gave a wink with the eye on the side away from the outlaws, there was not even the slightest suggestion that her motives had been understood by Madam Bulldog. Instead, the blonde was watching her with a blank and yet unnerving intensity such as she had seen when top male gun fighters were facing an enemy. Was it possible, she wondered, that the woman for whom she had developed such a liking and respect believed she was serious and seeking to avenge the defeat she had suffered.

'One!' Cousins announced, but he did not intend to hurry the count. Wanting to savour the enjoyment of watching two women prepared to kill one another, he continued slowly, 'Two! Three!'

Such was the silence which had descended over the bar-room, every male eye being fixed upon Calamity and Madam, the call of a whippoorwill sounded clearly from the alley outside the saloon.

'Now!' the red head hissed.

Saying the word, Calamity began to pivot away from the counter with her right hand turning palm outwards to close around the ivory butt of her Colt. Even as she did so, she was aware of the danger. If the blonde had misread her intentions, she would damned soon suffer the consequences and her life expectancy would be *very* short. To make things worse, having shot down the girl who was trying to save her, Madam would almost certainly be killed by the outlaws.

Regardless of her behaviour, the blonde had guessed what Calamity had in mind. While feeling the girl was ill-advised to make such a play, she was ready to back it 'up to the Green River' as the old saying went. She had sensed the conern she was causing as a result of her apparent lack of comprehension, but had not wished to endanger their far from extensive chances by offering a warning to the watching outlaws.

Accepting there was a good reason for the command being given at that particular point in the counting, Madam acted upon it with great promptitude. Commencing her draw and turning outwards, she was an instant after the red head in making the movements. For all that, the Webley was out of her holster and roared before the Navy Colt spoke in

Calamity's right hand. The interval between the shots was of a sufficient duration for the blonde to have beaten the red head to the draw by a margin which ruled out any advantage needing to be gained through the barrel of the weapon being shorter.

Unfortunately, having been confident this was one occasion when she could better the buxom woman—her weapon being longer notwithstanding—Calamity selected the same target. Following on the heels of the .450 Eley bullet, her .36 calibre ball of soft lead also struck Frank Cousins in the left side of the chest. However, while that fired by Madam pierced his heart, her load went an inch to the right of that vital organ. Even in the extreme urgency of the situation, seeing the result, she realized that once again the blonde had proven to be best.

There was, however, no time for disappointment or congratulations!

Taken unawares, the outlaws did not respond immediately to the unexpected development. Then, with the lifeless body of their leader pitching backwards from amongst them, even Mortimer Cousins joined them in grabbing for guns. Before any could clear leather, there was a distraction. From upstairs came the double roar of the twin loads of a shotgun being discharged. These were followed by the scream of a man in mortal agony and two thuds caused by heavy objects crashing to the floor. Regardless of the suggestion that their companions sent to kill the marshal had been prevented in no uncertain fashion, only the lawyer failed to resume the interrupted attempts to bring out revolvers.

Knowing the affair was still far from over, Madam was ready to sell her life as dearly as possible. While preparing to continue shooting, resigned to there being no hope of surviving against so many men, she wished there was some way Calamity could avoid the same fate.

Although the blonde was not responsible, the means were provided!

The door on the side of the bar-room from which the call of the whippoorwill had sounded was thrown open!

Three armed men burst in!

Having been assisted by Trudeau Front de Boeuf through the escape route he had created, Mark Counter had wasted no time in asking how the other came to be there at such an opportune moment. Instead, he had helped the elderly deputy to leave and led the way to the rear entrance. The door was locked, but was forced open more quietly than if it had been kicked, by the combined pressure of the two exceptionally powerful cousins. Collecting his gunbelt from the office, where he had been compelled to leave it when captured, the blond giant had set free the other prisoners brought by the Tennyson Regulators. Telling them to wait until they heard shooting before leaving the jailhouse, he had set out with Front de Boeuf and Hoscroft—who had also retrieved full armament—in the direction of the Hide And Horn Saloon. They had seen Calamity going in through the kitchen door on making their escape and hoped she could help prevent the outlaws from killing Madam Bulldog and the marshal until they were able to intervene.

Having given a signal it was hoped Calamity would understand, the rescuers had been on the point of entering when the shooting took place!

Fanning apart, the three men opened fire!

Mark had an Army Colt in each hand, and was using them with deadly skill!

Even more lethally effective was the Greener whipit gun and sawed-off shotgun held by Front de Boeuf and Hoscroft!

While any bullet fired by the blond giant would strike only a single target, the spreading clouds of buckshot balls from each of the four barrels could reach more than one objective!

Caught in the swathe of flying lead, its volume augmented by the discharging of Madam's Webley and Calamity's Navy Colt, the men who had accompanied Frank Cousins on the mission of vengeance suffered grievously from the opening volley. All except one of them were struck somewhere or other by either bullets or smaller buckshot balls. So devastating was the result, there was not even one shot fired in return.

By some quirk of fate, Mortimer Cousins had escaped

180

unscathed. Not for long, however. Knowing the lawyer would be able to implicate himself and his mother of their part in what had happened, Front de Boeuf was determined this should not be allowed. Dropping the empty whipit gun, he twisted the Army Colt free from his waist band and raised it to eye level at arms' length. Employing a double handed grip to make sure of his aim, he sent a bullet into the centre of Cousins' forehead an instant before a declaration of surrender could be made.

Even as the massive young man fired, Mark and Hoscroft, the latter also having exchanged his shotgun for a Colt, finished off two of the survivors who were offering signs of showing fight. Outside, seeing armed men pouring from the jailhouse, the outlaws left to keep watch mounted their horses and took flight.

With a feeling of relief, as he was glancing around, Front de Boeuf discovered not one member of the Cousins' clan was left alive. Knowing their leader had never made a habit of taking anybody except members of the family into his confidence, the young man felt sure there would be no danger of betrayal from any outlaw taken prisoner.

Studying the scene with an equal satisfaction, Mark and Hoscroft saw it in a different light to Front de Boeuf!

In a matter of seconds, the Cousins gang which had long exercised a reign of terror throughout much of Texas had ceased to exist!

'Are you all right?' the blond giant asked, swinging to look at the blonde and the red head.

'Nope,' Calamity replied. 'I had the shit scared out of me when I reckoned Madam hadn't cottoned on to what I was doing and was set to throw down on me.'

'Go on,' the blonde answered. 'I thought you could take a joke!'

'And I can,' the red head declared. 'What's more, we don't need to have no shooting match. I know now you're faster'n a better shot than me and let it not be said lil ole Martha Jane Canary's scared to—!'

'What was that name you said?' Madam gasped.

181

'Martha Jane Canary,' Calamity supplied. 'I reckon my folks must've had a dis—!'

'Oh my god!' the blonde croaked and, her face losing all its colour, she crumpled limply to the floor.

'I didn't know she was hit!' Mark said worriedly.

'She wasn't!' Calamity stated, dropping to her knees alongside the woman. After making an examination, she looked up with puzzlement etched upon her face. 'Hell's fires, boys. Happen I didn't reckon its something this spunky lady'd never do, I'd swear she's gone and throwed a faint!'

* * *

'Those of Gilmore's bunch who could've 'lit a shuck out of Tennyson,' Mark Counter reported, visiting his uncle at noon on the day after the defeat of the Cousins' gang. 'And I don't reckon any of them'll be coming back, even to sell off their businesses or to collect anything they've left behind. Cousin Trudeau said for me to tell you Aunt Jessica don't feel comfortable here, so he won't be stopping for the big poker game at the Hide And Horn. They're leaving tomorrow morning. Pockets allows he can hold down the town until you're up and about again.'

'He can at that,' Collier confirmed. 'So you can head back to Fort Worth as soon as you've a mind.'

'That's something else I wanted to tell you,' the blond giant replied. 'I've just now got a telegraph message from Dusty saying Lawyer Benskin dropped by at the OD Connected to see Ole Devil and allows he never sent for me to meet him in Cowtown.'

'The hell you say!' the peace officer ejaculated, sitting a little straighter in bed and looking far better than when his nephew had arrived in Tennyson. 'Do you reckon Jessica and Cyrus had anything to do with it?'

'How do you mean?'

'You was got to Cowtown by a fake message, which brought you here and mixed you in a fuss that could've wound up with you made wolf bait. Should that have

182

happened, they'd stand a chance of winding up with Aunt Cornelia's money. Which could mean they know more than they should about what's been happening around here.'

'Family always thinks the worse of them,' Mark drawled tolerantly. 'Hell, Uncle Tune, Tru likely stopped me getting killed by Gilmore and his *amigo* while I was getting out of the jailhouse, and him and Aunt Jessica had come to pry me loose so we could save you. I reckon you've got them all wrong.'

'Likely,' Collier conceded. 'Hell, it must be getting shot, my notion's so full of holes I'd've laughed my head off happen anybody else had given it to me.'

Before any more could be said, the door opened. Followed by Calamity, Madam Bulldog entered the room. Studying her, Mark decided she looked recovered from the still unexplained shock which had caused her to faint the previous evening. On recovering, she had asked the red head to accompany her to her living accommodation and neither had put in an appearance until their arrival in Tune's room.

'Just dropped by to tell you I'm pulling out,' Calamity announced. 'Hey though, I know now why Madam here could lick me at poker playing, cussing, drinking, fighting tooth 'n' claw and using a gun.'

'How's that, Calam?' Collier inquired.

'She's my maw is why!' the girl replied, looking at the blonde with admiration and open affection.

'Your *maw*?' the marshal repeated, as he and his nephew alternated gazes between Madam and Calamity.

'My maw,' the red head confirmed.

'Aren't you staying on with her?' the blond giant asked.

'Shucks, no!' Calamity replied, hugging the smiling woman. 'We're too much alike to live peaceable under the same roof. So maw's given back all she took me for at poker and I'm headed back to join Dobe and the outfit.'

'She's going to come and visit me for a spell, though,' Madam went on.

'That's *bueno*,' Collier enthused. 'Only I'd be obliged happen you'd do me a favour. Wait until I'm fit enough to get the hell out of Tennyson before you pair get together again.'

In Conclusion

Our readers may have been puzzled, as we were when working on the manuscript for the narrative from which this volume is an 'expansion', by certain inexplicable aspects of the plot.

For example, we had become impressed by the competence, ability and acumen of Madam Bulldog. Therefore, we found it hard to understand why she would allow herself to be provoked into a fist fight—with the attendant danger of suffering an incapacitating injury—*after* the killing of Brock Cousins and knowing his family were going to seek revenge. We also felt it difficult to accept that, hot-headed and impetuous though she undoubtedly was, Martha 'Calamity Jane' Canary would be so irresponsible as to seek such a confrontation with a woman she had come to admire under those circumstances.

Furthermore, the 'motivation' of the movie, HIGH NOON, notwithstanding, we considered it unlikely the citizens of a Western town—in which the majority of the population had grown up handling firearms—would take so calmly and meekly the arrival of a comparatively small band of outlaws. They would, we concluded, have needed some very powerful inducement to behave in such a fashion.

We also had been puzzled by references to somebody called 'Beef Head'—one English translation of 'Front de Boeuf'—in various documents put at our disposal by members of the Counter family. Seeking enlightenment, we were at last granted permission to produce this volume and others which will be forthcoming describing the activities of two bearers of that name.

Lastly, we wonder whether the source from which we obtained details for use in the original version had solved the mystery and, being refused permission to disclose the findings, sought to draw attention to the matter by calling the Hide And Horn Saloon the 'Bull's Head'?

Appendix One

With his exceptional good looks and magnificent physical development—which might have qualified him for a 'Mr. Universe' title if such competitions were held in his day —Mark Counter presented the kind of appearance which many people expected of his better known *amigo*, Captain Dustine Edward Marsden 'Dusty' Fog. It was a fact of which they took advantage when the need arose.[1] On one occasion, however, although the intended victim was the Rio Hondo gun wizard, this misapprehension was the cause of the blond giant being subjected to an attempted murder.[2]

While serving under the command of Brigadier General Bushrod Sheldon as a lieutenant during the War Between The States, Mark's merits as an efficient and courageous officer were overshadowed by his unconventional taste in uniforms. Always a dandy and coming from a very wealthy family, he was able to indulge his whims in that respect. Despite considerable opposition and disapproval on the part of hide-bound senior officers, his selection of a skirtless tunic in particular came to be much copied by the other young bloods in the Army of the Confederate States' Cavalry. Similarly, having been granted independent means via the will of a maiden aunt,[3] his taste in attire made him the arbiter of fashion among the hard-working, harder-playing cowhands of Texas.

When peace came, or rather a cessation of military hostilities,[4] Mark accompanied Sheldon and his regiment to serve the Emperor Maximilian. There he had his first meeting with Dusty Fog[5] and the Ysabel Kid,[6] helping them accomplish a mission upon the result of which hung the future relations between the United States of America and Mexico. On returning to Texas with them, he was invited to work for Dusty's best known uncle—General Jackson Baines 'Ole Devil' Hardin, C.S.A.[7]—as a member of the OD Connected ranch's floating outfit.[8] Knowing his two older brothers could help his father, Big Ranse, to run the R Over C ranch in the Big Bend country—and suspecting life would in all probability prove more exciting in the company of his two *amigos* —he had accepted.

An expert cowhand, Mark soon became known as Dusty's 'right bower'.[9] He also gained considerable acclaim by virtue of his tremendous strength—which helped him to raise the wagon of Miss Martha 'Calamity Jane' Canary singlehanded after a wheel had sunk and been trapped in a gopher hole,[10] then later to break the neck of a longhorn bull with his bare hands[11]—and ability in a rough-house brawl. However, being so much in the company of Dusty Fog, his full potential as a gun fighter received less attention. Men who were best competent to judge such matters claimed that, whether using a brace of Colt 1860 Army Model revolvers,[12] or their famed successors, 'Peacemakers' with Cavalry Model barrels,[13], [13a], [13b] he was second only to the Rio Hondo gun wizard in speed and accuracy. This was, in fact, proven in competition during the First Cochise County Fair, where he too beat a number of men prominent in the annals of Western gun play.[14]

Many women found Mark irresistible, including Calamity Jane, *q.v.* However, in his younger days, only one—the lady outlaw, Belle Starr[15]—held his heart.[16] It was not until several years after her death that the match making by the wife of Dusty Fog[17] and Betty Raybold, née Hardin,[18] led him to court and marry Dawn Sutherland. Although there had been no romance between them at the time, they first met on the trail drive taken by Colonel Charles Goodnight[19] to Fort Sumner, New Mexico.[20] The discovery of vast oil deposits on their land brought an added wealth to them and forms a major part of the income for the present day members of the family.[21] Three descendants of Mark, each of whom inherited his handsome features and physique, have achieved considerable fame on their own account.[22]

1. One occasion is described in: THE SOUTH WILL RISE AGAIN.

2. The incident is recorded in: BEGUINAGE.

3. One result of the bequest is described in: Part Two, 'We Hang Horse Thieves High', J.T.'S HUNDREDTH.

4. An ironic note is that, due to the slowness of communications having delayed the arrival of the news, troops under the command of Colonel John Salmon 'Rip' Ford won for the South the final battle of the War Between The States at Palmitto Hill, some fifteen miles east of Brownsville, Cameron County, Texas, on May the 13th, 1865, more than a month after the surrender of General Robert E. Lee on behalf of the Confederate States at the Appomattox Courthouse on the 9th of April should have brought an end to all military hostilities between the South and the North.

5. Details of the careers and special qualifications of Captain Dustine Edward Marsden 'Dusty' Fog and the Ysabel Kid can be found in various volumes of the Civil War *and* Floating Outfit *series.*

6. Told in: THE YSABEL KID.

7. Details of the Career and special qualifications of General Jackson Baines 'Ole Devil' Hardin, C.S.A., are given in the Ole Devil Hardin *series,* Part Four, 'Mr. Colt's Revolving Cylinder Pistol', J.T.'S HUNDREDTH —all of which cover his younger period—and Floating Outfit *series. How he was crippled and left confined to a wheelchair shortly after the end of the War Between The States is described in* 'The Paint' *episode of* THE FASTEST GUN IN TEXAS *and his death is recorded in:* DOC LEROY, M.D. *The General's sobriquet arose partly from his having enhanced the Mephistophelian aspects of his features in early life and because his contemporaries said he was 'a lil ole devil for a fight'.*

8. 'Floating outfit': a group of four to six cowhands employed by a large ranch to work the most distant sections of its range. Taking food in a chuckwagon, or 'greasy sack' on the back of a mule, depending upon the intended length of their absence, they would be away from the ranch house for several days at a time. For this reason, they were selected from the most competent and trustworthy members of the crew. Due to the prominence of General Hardin in the affairs of Texas, which the injury we referred to in Footnote 7 did not diminish despite restricting his personal participation, the floating outfit of the OD Connected ranch were frequently sent to assist such of his friends who found themselves in difficulty or endangered.

9. 'Right bower': colloquial name for a second-in-command, deriving from the title of the second highest trump card in the game of euchre.

10. Described in: Part One, 'The Bounty On Belle Starr's Scalp',

TROUBLED RANGE *and its 'expansion'*, CALAMITY, MARK AND BELLE.

11. Told in: THE MAN FROM TEXAS. *When preparing the manuscript for this episode in 1965, we gave it the far more apt title,* ROUNDUP CAPTAIN, *but the publishers at that time made the substitution without consulting us or offering any explanation for his decision.*

12. Although members of the military sometimes claimed—perhaps tongue in cheek—it was easier to kill a sailor than a soldier, the weight factor of the respective revolvers caused the United States' Navy to adopt one with a calibre of .36 of an inch while the Army selected the heavier .44. The weapon would be carried on the belt of a seaman and not—handguns have been originally and primarily developed for use by cavalry—on the person who would be doing most of his travelling and fighting from the back of a horse. Therefore, throughout the latter half of the Nineteenth Century, .44 was referred to as the 'Army' and .36 as the 'Navy' calibre.

13. Introduced in 1871, as the Colt Model P 'Single Action Army' Model —although its original calibre was .45 and not .44—the revolver became more popularly known as the 'Peacemaker'. Production continued until 1941, when it was taken out of the line to make way for production of the more modern types of weapons required in World War II. In 1955, popular demand—said to have been created by interest in the numerous action-escapism-adventure Western series on television—brought the Peacemaker back into production and it is still on the line.

13a. During the first production period, over three hundred and fifty thousand *Peacemakers were manufactured. They were chambered for practically every handgun calibre—with the exception of the .41 and .44 Magnums, which were not commercially developed until later—from .22 Short Rimfire to .476 Eley. Those chambered for the .44-40 Centre-Fire cartridge used in the Winchester Model of 1873 rifle and carbine, allowing the ammunition to be interchangeable, were called the 'Frontier' Model.*

13b. The barrels lengths of the Peacemaker could be from three inches in the 'Storekeeper' Model, which did not have an extractor rod, to sixteen inches in the so-called 'Buntline Special'. The latter was also offered with an attachable metal 'skeleton' butt stock so it could be used as an extemporized carbine. However, the main barrel lengths were: Civilian, four and three-quarter inches; Artillery, five and a half inches; Cavalry, seven and a half inches.

14. Told in: GUN WIZARD.

15. We have occasionally been asked why the 'Belle Starr' we describe is so different from the photographs which appear in various books. The researches of fictionist-genealogist, Philip José Farmer—author of, among numerous other works, TARZAN ALIVE, A Definitive Biography Of Lord Greystoke *and* DOC SAVAGE, His Apocalyptic Life—*with whom we consulted, have established that the lady to whom we refer is not the same person as an equally famous bearer of the name. However, the present day members of the Counter family have asked that we and Mr. Farmer keep her true identity a secret and we intend to do so.*

16. How Mark Counter's romance with Belle Starr began, progressed and was brought to an end is told in: Part One, 'The Bounty On Belle Starr's Scalp', TROUBLED RANGE, *its 'expansion'*, CALAMITY, MARK AND BELLE, Mark's section of J.T.'S HUNDREDTH, THE BAD BUNCH, THE GENTLE GIANT, RANGELAND HERCULES, Part Four, 'A Lady Known As Belle', THE HARD RIDERS *and* GUNS IN THE NIGHT. *Belle also makes 'guest' appearances in:* HELL IN THE PALO DURO, GO BACK TO HELL, Part Six, 'Mrs. Wild Bill', J.T.'S LADIES *and* WACO'S BADGE *and 'stars' in:* WANTED, BELLE STARR.

17. Lady Winifred Amelia 'Freddie Woods' Besgrove-Woodstole. How she met Dusty Fog and their romance progressed is told in: THE MAKING OF A LAWMAN, THE TROUBLE BUSTERS, THE GENTLE GIANT *and* THE FORTUNE HUNTERS. *She also makes 'guest' appearances in:* WHITE STALLION, RED MARE; THE WHIP AND THE WAR LANCE *and* Part Five, 'The Butcher's Fiery End', J.T.'s LADIES. *However, the present day members of the Hardin, Fog and Blaze clan will not supply the details of why she—having been born into one of Britain's oldest and most aristocratic families—elected to live under an assumed name in the United States of America. Nor was Mrs. Jack Tragg, formerly the Right Honourable Brenda Besgrove-Woodstole—who makes a 'guest' appearance in,* THE LAWMEN OF ROCKABYE COUNTY—*any more inclined to be informative when we raised the matter with her on our last meeting.*

18. Alvin Dustine 'Cap' Fog and other members of the clan with whom we have been in contact cannot, or will not, *make any statement upon the exact relationship between Elizabeth 'Betty' and her 'grandfather' General Ole Devil Hardin,* q.v. *She appears in:* Part Five, 'A Time For Improvisation, Mr. Blaze', J.T.'S HUNDREDTH; Part Four, 'It's Our Turn To Improvise, Miss Blaze', J.T.'S LADIES; KILL DUSTY FOG!; THE BAD BUNCH; McGRAW'S INHERITANCE: Part Two, 'The Quartet', THE HALF BREED; MASTER OF TRIGGERNOMETRY; THE RIO HONDO WAR *and* GUNSMOKE THUNDER.

19. The honorific 'Colonel' given to Charles Goodnight was not a military rank, but granted as a tribute to his integrity, ability of fighting man and leader. As is told in various volumes of the Alvin Dustine 'Cap' Fog series, Dusty Fog acquired a similar title later in his career. The Colonel makes 'guest' appearances in: GOODNIGHT'S DREAM, FROM HIDE AND HORN, SET TEXAS BACK ON HER FEET, SIDEWINDER *and* THE MAN FROM TEXAS.

20. Told in: GOODNIGHT'S DREAM (*Bantam Books U.S.A. 1974 edition re-titled,* THE FLOATING OUTFIT, *despite Transworld Publishers having brought out a book with that title*) *and* FROM HIDE AND HORN.

21. This is established by inference in: Part Three, 'The Deadly Ghost', YOU'RE A TEXAS RANGER, ALVIN FOG.

22. *Three of Mark's most prominent descendants, for whom we have the honour to be biographer, are:*

a. Ranse Andrew Smith, grandson, formerly a sergeant of Company 'Z', Texas Rangers, who makes his first appearance in: THE JUSTICE OF COMPANY 'Z'.

b. Bradford Mark 'Brad' Counter, great grandson, serving as a deputy sheriff in Rockabye County, Texas. His career as a peace officer is recorded in the Rockabye County *series and* Part Eleven, 'Preventive Law Enforcement', J.T.'S HUNDREDTH. *He also makes a 'guest' appearance in* Part Three, 'A Contract For Alice Fayde', J.T.'S LADIES. *All these volumes cover various aspects of law enforcement in present day Texas.*

c. James Allenvale 'Bunduki' Gunn, great grandson, formerly chief warden of the Ambagasali Wild Life Reserve, details of whose career can be found in: Part Twelve, *and the various volumes of the* Bunduki *series. His sobriquet is a pun on the Swahili word for a hand-held firearm of any kind being* 'Bunduki'. *He also makes a 'guest' appearance in:* Part Three, 'Death To Simba Nyeuse': J.T.'S LADIES.

Appendix Two

Deserted by her husband, Charlotte Canary decided the best way she could assure a future for her children was to leave them in a convent at St. Louis and head west to seek her fortune. However, there had been far too much of her lively, reckless spirit in her eldest daughter, Martha Jane, for the scheme to be entirely successful. Rebelling against the strict life imposed by the nuns, the girl celebrated her sixteenth birthday by running away. Hiding in one of the freight wagons owned by Cecil 'Dobe' Killem, she had travelled some twelve miles from the city before being discovered. She might have been sent back, but the cook for the outfit was too drunk to work. One of the things which the girl had been taught at the convent was good, if plain, cooking. The meal she produced was so well received that Killem had yielded to her request to be taken to Wichita, Kansas, where she claimed to have an aunt who would give her a home. In later years, she would claim her intention was to search for her mother.

During the journey to Wichita, raiding Sioux warriors who had wiped out two other freight outfits failed to locate Killem's wagons. What was more, the goods they carried were sold so advantageously the whole crew received a bonus and their employer was offered a lucrative contract to deliver goods further west. Learning the 'aunt' was no more than a figment of the girl's imagination and regarding her as a good luck charm, the drivers had prevailed upon Killem to let her travel with them. Not that he, having taken a liking to her for her spunky and cheerful nature, took much persuading and she had been just as willing to go along.

At first, known as 'Martha', wearing male clothing for convenience, the girl had helped the cook and performed other menial duties around the camp. She had soon graduated to driving and, proving a quick learner, in a short while there was little she could not do in that line of work. Not only could she harness and drive the six horse team of a Conestoga wagon, she carried out the maintenance of the vehicle and cared for the needs of the team well enough to satisfy Killem's exacting requirements. She was taught to use a long lashed bull whip as an inducement to the team's activity, or as an effective weapon, to handle firearms with skill and generally fend for herself on the open plains whether travelling with a wagon train, or making deliveries alone.

Visiting saloons with the rest of the outfit, the girl was frequently called upon to defend herself against the objections of such female employees who objected to her trespassing upon what they considered to be their own domain. Leading a much more active life than her assailants and having been taught masculine rather than feminine methods of attack and defense, she had had an advantage over them. In fact—although the lady outlaw, Belle Starr, q.v., had held her to a hard fought draw when they first met[1]—up to the events recorded in this volume, she had never been defeated.

Courageous, loyal to her friends, happy-go-lucky and generous to such an extent that she had deliberately lost her share in a saloon she had inherited jointly with a professional gambler, Frank Derringer,[2] the girl had developed a penchant for becoming involved in dangerous and precarious situations. Visiting New Orleans, she acted as a decoy to lure the Strangler, a notorious mass murderer of young women, to his doom.[3] While helping deliver supplies to an Army post, she fought with a professional female pugilist and went to the rescue of an officer captured by Indians.[4] In the Lone Star State, she helped Texas Ranger Danny Fog[5] to stamp out a wave of cattle rustling which was threatening to cause a range war.[6] What started out as a peaceful journey as a passenger on a stagecoach ended with her acting as driver and taking part in the capture of the criminals who robbed it.[7] Going to visit a ranch which was left to her by her father, accompanied by the Ysabel Kid, *q.v.*, she was nearly killed when a rival claimant had her fastened to a log which was to be sent through a circular saw.[8] She helped Belle Starr, Betty Hardin, *q.v.*, and Belle 'the Rebel Spy' Boyd[9] bring an end to the nefarious career of a gang of murderous women outlaws.[10] In the company of Belle Boyd and Captain Patrick 'The Remittance Kid' Reeder,[11] she took part in averting an uprising of Canadian Indians and *Meti*.[12] Taking part in a hunting trip with an aristocratic Englishman, she and his sister had been kidnapped.[13]

Among her many friends, the girl counted the members of General Jackson Baines 'Ole Devil' Hardin's floating outfit. She was on particularly intimate terms with Mark Counter, *q.v.* However, on one memorable occasion, she posed as the wife of its leader, Captain Dustine Edward Marsden 'Dusty' Fog and assisted him in dealing with a bunch of land grabbers.[14] Other close acquaintances were James Butler 'Wild Bill' Hickok and his wife[15] and she captured his murderer on the day he was killed.[16]

Because of her penchant for finding trouble and becoming involved in brawls, the girl soon acquired the sobriquet by which she would become famous throughout the West and, in the course of time, elsewhere in the world.

People called her 'Calamity Jane'.

1. The clash was described in, Part One, 'The Bounty On Belle Starr's Scalp', TROUBLED RANGE *and amended, as a result of further information having been forthcoming, in:* CALAMITY, MARK AND BELLE.

2. Told in: COLD DECK, HOT LEAD.

3. Told in: THE BULL WHIP BREED.

4. Told in: TROUBLE TRAIL.

5. Danny Fog was the younger brother of Captain Dustine Edward Marsden 'Dusty' Fog. How he met his death is told in: A TOWN CALLED YELLOWDOG.

6. Told in: THE COW THIEVES.

7. Told in: CALAMITY SPELLS TROUBLE.

8. Told in: WHITE STALLION, RED MARE.

9. *Details of the career of Belle 'the Rebel Spy' Boyd are given in:* A MATTER OF HONOUR; THE COLT AND THE SABRE; THE REBEL SPY; THE BLOODY BORDER; BACK TO THE BLOODY BORDER —*Berkley Books, U.S.A., 1978 edition re-titled,* RENEGADE—THE HOODED RIDERS; THE BAD BUNCH; SET A-FOOT; TO ARMS! TO ARMS! IN DIXIE!; THE SOUTH WILL RISE AGAIN; Part Eight, 'Affair Of Honour', J.T.'S HUNDREDTH; THE QUEST FOR BOWIE'S BLADE; THE REMITTANCE KID; THE WHIP AND THE WAR LANCE *and* Part Five, 'The Butcher's Fiery End', J.T.'S LADIES.

10. *Told in:* THE BAD BUNCH.

11. *The researches of fictionist-genealogist Philip José Farmer,* q.v., *have established that Captain (later Major General) Patrick Reeder (K.C.B., V.C., D.S.O., M.C. and Bar) was the uncle of the celebrated British detective, Mr. J.G. Reeder, whose biography is recorded in:* ROOM 13, THE MIND OF MR. J.G. REEDER, RED ACES, MR. J.G. REEDER RETURNS *and* TERROR KEEP by Edgar Wallace *and whose organization plays a prominent part in the events recorded in:* CAP FOG, TEXAS RANGER, MEET MR. J.G. REEDER.

12. *Told in:* THE WHIP AND THE WAR LANCE.

13. *Told in:* THE BIG HUNT.

14. *Told in:* Part Two, 'A Wife For Dusty Fog', THE SMALL TEXAN.

15. *Details of how Miss Martha 'Calamity Jane' Canary made the acquaintance of the wife of James Butler 'Wild Bill' Hickok are given in:* Part Six, 'Mrs. Wild Bill', J.T.'S LADIES.

16. *Told in:* Part Seven, 'Deadwood, August 2nd, 1876', J.T.'S HUNDREDTH.

Appendix Three

During the years we have been writing, we have frequently received letters asking for various Western terms, or incidents to which we refer, to be explained in greater detail. While we do not have the slightest objections to receiving such mail, we have found it saves much time-consuming repetition to include those most often requested in each volume. Our 'old hands' have seen them before, but there are always 'new chums' coming along who may not have.

1. Although Americans in general used the word 'cinch', derived from the Spanish, 'cincha', for the short band made from coarsely woven horsehair, canvas, or cordage and terminated at each end with a metal ring which —together with the latigo—*is used to fasten the saddle on the back of a horse, because of its Mexican connotations, Texans employ the term 'girth', generally pronouncing it 'girt'. As cowhands of the Lone Star State fastened the end of the lariat to the saddlehorn when roping the half wild longhorn cattle, or free-ranging mustangs, instead of using a 'dally' which could be slipped free almost instantaneously in an emergency, their rigs had two girths for added security.*

2. 'Light a shuck', cowhands' expression for leaving, usually hurriedly. It derives from the practise in the night camps of trail drives, or roundups on the open range of supplying 'shucks'—dried corn cobs—to be lit and used as illumination by anybody who had to leave the camp-fire and walk in the darkness. As the 'shuck' burned away very quickly, a person wanting to benefit from its light had to move with some speed.

3. 'Make wolf bait': one Western term meaning to kill. It had its origins in the habit amongst ranchers, when a range had become infested by predators —not necessarily just wolves, as black and grizzly bears were just as likely to develop a taste for such easily acquired food—of slaughtering an animal and, having poisoned the carcase, leaving it to be found and devoured.

4. We strongly suspect that the trend in film and television Westerns made since the early 1960's, whereby all cowhands are portrayed as long haired, heavily bearded and filthy, stems less from a desire of the production companies to create 'realism' than because there were so few actors —particularly those to play supporting roles—who were short haired and clean shaven, also because the 'liberal' elements who had begun to gain control of the entertainment media appear to have an obsession for exhibiting filthy habits, obscene language, dirty conditions and appearances. In our extensive reference library, we cannot find a dozen photographs of actual cowhands—as opposed to old time gold prospectors, mountain men, or Army scouts—with long hair and bushy beards. In fact, our reading on the subject has led us to assume the term 'long hair' was one of opprobrium in the cattle country of the Old West and Prohibition era, as it still is today.

5. The sharp toes and high heels of the boots worn by cowhands are purely functional. The former could find and enter, or be slipped from a stirrup iron very quickly in an emergency. Not only did the latter offer a firmer grip in the stirrups, they could be spiked into the ground to supply extra holding power when roping on foot.

6. 'Gone to Texas': at odds with the law, usually in the United States of America at the time the saying came into being. Many fugitives from justice entered Texas during the colonization period—which was commenced in the early 1820's due to the Government of Mexico offering grants of land to 'Anglos' so they could act as a 'buffer state' against the marauding Comanche, Waco and other Indian tribes—and continued until annexation as a State of the Union on February the 16th, 1846. Until the latter became a fact, such miscreants as had arrived had known there was little danger of being arrested and extradited by the local authorities. In fact, as was said to be the case in Kenya from the early 1920's until the outbreak of World War II—in spite of the great number of honest, law-abiding and hard working people who genuinely wished to make their home there—Texas in the days before independence was attained from Mexican domination and during the short period as a self governing Republic, which became a fact after their decisive victory at the Battle of San Jacinto on April the 21st, 1836, gained a reputation for being 'a place in the sun for shady people'.

7. 'Give it up to the Green River': another term meaning to kill, generally with some form of edged weapon. First produced at a factory on the Green River, at Green Field, Massachusetts, in 1834, a very popular brand of knife had the following inscription on the blade just below the hilt, 'J. Russell & Co./Green River Works'. Any weapon thrust into an enemy 'up to the Green River' would almost certainly inflict a fatal wound whether it bore the inscription or not.

8. 'Mason-Dixon' line, also erroneously called the 'Mason-Dixie' line: the boundary between Maryland and Pennsylvania, as surveyed during 1763 –67 by Englishmen, Charles Mason and Jeremiah Dixon, which came to be regarded as the dividing line separating the Southern 'Slave' and the Northern 'Free' States of the Union.

9. 'New England': the North-East section of the United States of America, including Massachusetts, New Hampshire, Maine, Vermont, Connecticut and Rhode Island, which was first primarily settled by people from the British Isles. Citizens of New England acquired a reputation of being dour and hard-headed businessmen.

10. In the Old West, the jurisdiction of various types of law enforcement agencies was established as follows: town marshal, sometimes called 'constable' in smaller places, confined to the town or city which hired him; sheriff, to his own county, although in less heavily populated areas he might also serve as marshal of the county seat; Texas and Arizona Rangers could go anywhere in their respective State, but the former were technically required to await an invitation by the appropriate local authority before participating in an investigation; United States' marshal had jurisdiction anywhere in the country, but was only intended to become involved in 'Federal' crimes.

11. 'Clip point' bladed knife: one where the last few inches of the otherwise unsharpened back of the blade joins and becomes an extension of the main cutting surface in a concave arc. This is the characteristic which identifies all 'bowie' knives. A 'spear' point, which is less utilitarian and employed on pure fighting rather than general purpose knives, is formed by the two sharpened sides coming together centrally in symmetrical curves.

If you have enjoyed reading this book and other works by the same author, why not join

THE J.T. EDSON APPRECIATION SOCIETY

You will receive a signed photograph of J.T. Edson, bimonthly Newsletters giving details of all new books and re-prints of earlier titles.

Competitions with autographed prizes to be won in every issue of the Edson Newsletter.

A chance to meet J.T. Edson.

Send S.A.E. for details and membership form to:

The Secretary,
J.T. Edson Appreciation Society,
P.O. Box 13,
MELTON MOWBRAY,
Leics.